MW00752497

**The sax sizzle**
**them in a sensual cocoon, a world of their own**

It was as if time stopped, along with Diamond's rational thinking. Because for the life of her, she couldn't think of anything more logical to do than to kiss those lips, to crush the nipples that were even now hardening at the mere thought of being touched against Jackson's hard chest.

She took a step.

Jackson's eyes narrowed as he watched her come closer. He looked at her lips, slightly parted with desire. Wanting him was written all over her face. His message was being proclaimed from an area decidedly lower, by a rapidly increasing bulge in the front of his jeans.

He took a step.

They now stood just inches apart, neither moving, barely breathing. At the risk of having to fire himself for insubordination, Jackson reached out and ran a finger along Diamond's jawline. His touch was more electric than the guitar that now accompanied the sax. She licked her lips and suppressed a shiver. He watched, wondering how they tasted, those lips, wanting to know how she tasted. Her eyes flickered shut, and then back open, even as her head tilted seemingly of its own accord. To hell with stalking ex-coworkers and iron-clad declarations. He would be a rule-breaker. Thoughts of consequences could come later. Right now all he wanted were her lips. On his. Now! He bent his head down. One more step and the kiss would begin. Just one more step....

**Books by Zuri Day**

Kimani Romance

*Diamond Dreams*

---

### ZURI DAY

snuck her first Harlequin romance novel at the age of twelve from her older sister's off-limits collection and was hooked from page one. Knights in shining armor and happily-ever-afters filled her teen years and spurred a life-long love of reading. That she now creates these stories as a full-time author is a dream come true! Splitting her time between the stunning Caribbean islands and Southern California, she's always busy writing her next novel, Zuri makes time to connect with readers and meet with book clubs. She'd love to hear from you, and personally answers every email that's sent to Zuri@ZuriDay.com.

# DIAMOND
# Dreams

# ZURI DAY

KIMANI™
ROMANCE

If you purchased this book without a cover you should be aware
that this book is stolen property. It was reported as "unsold and
destroyed" to the publisher, and neither the author nor the
publisher has received any payment for this "stripped book."

To all the readers, far and near,
I raise my glass and toast with cheer!

May your dreams come true, your smile remain,
and your life be as bubbly as a fine champagne!

KIMANI PRESS™

ISBN-13: 978-0-373-86253-5

Recycling programs
for this product may
not exist in your area.

DIAMOND DREAMS

Copyright © 2012 by Lutishia Hinton

All rights reserved. The reproduction, transmission or utilization of this work
in whole or in part in any form by any electronic, mechanical or other means,
now known or hereafter invented, including xerography, photocopying and
recording, or in any information storage or retrieval system, is forbidden
without written permission. For permission please contact Kimani Press,
225 Duncan Mill Road, Toronto, Ontario M3B 3K9, Canada.

This is a work of fiction. Names, characters, places and incidents are
either the product of the author's imagination or are used fictitiously,
and any resemblance to actual persons, living or dead, business establishments,
events or locales is entirely coincidental.

® and TM are trademarks. Trademarks indicated with ® are registered in
the United States Patent and Trademark Office, the Canadian Trade Marks
Office and/or other countries.

www.kimanipress.com

Printed in U.S.A.

Dear Reader,

I am thrilled to introduce you to the Drakes of California!

When hearing the words *wine country,* most of us think of Napa Valley. So did I, until visiting Southern California's vineyards, a beautiful community surrounded by mountains, nestled midway between Los Angeles and San Diego. This picturesque setting (and a few glasses of wine) served to inspire this story about a dynasty using land that has been in the family for almost one hundred years! The Drake Vineyard is approximately sixty miles north of the first California grapes planted at Mission San Diego in 1769.

I love writing about strong women. Diamond Drake is all that and a glass of high-priced brut! She's used to being in control, which is why her irrepressible attraction to Jackson Wright is so exasperating. But we all know what happens when iron sharpens iron... sparks fly!

So, pour a glass of something delicious...and enjoy!

Zuri Day

To the wine country of Temecula, and especially winemaker David Vergari and media director Linda Kissam of Thornton Winery. The private tour and detail-laden interview were great, the wine…even better! And to my editor, Glenda Howard, who helped make this novel such a pleasure to write. La'Chaim!

## Chapter 1

"I'm proud of you, Diamond," Donald Drake said as he continued to flip through the latest report that she had provided. "The sketches are fantastic, and your attention to detail continues to be impressive. These innovative interior-design ideas are going to make ours one of the best resorts in California."

"One of the best resorts, period," Diamond corrected. "I told you that I could do it, Dad. I'm glad you trusted me with such a major aspect of our expansion." Diamond beamed from her father's words of praise. She considered herself the ultimate daddy's girl and never wanted to disappoint. And being the only girl in the family made her quite competitive with her two brothers for their father's attention.

"I don't know how much trust had to do with it," Dexter Drake drawled. Diamond's always lovable yet sometimes annoying younger brother reared back in his chair and placed his interlocked fingers behind his head. "I think it was all of that whining and begging you did that finally wore him down."

"I believe the correct verb is *negotiated,* dear brother. Mine was the best proposal submitted, period." Even as she said this, Diamond knew that there was a thread of truth to Dexter's statement. Her older brother, Donovan, handled most of the construction projects and had overseen the first phase of this one. It had taken a lot of research, idea submissions and—okay, maybe a little whining and begging—to convince Donald, the company's founder, board president and chief operating officer, that when it came to the interior-design work and final stages of construction for Drake Wines Resort & Spa, Diamond was the woman to oversee the job.

Dexter continued his needling. "Was it the best proposal? Or just the only one submitted twenty times?"

"Ha! Come on, Diamond. Fess up," Donovan said with a chuckle. "You did send that thing in several times."

"I sent in several addendums to keep everyone up-to-date on the evolving ideas and projections," Diamond retorted, with a tilt of her chin. "Which you would know, Mr. VP of Sales, if you pulled your head out of the books long enough to see what's happening with the rest of the company."

Donovan calmly rubbed his goatee. "I don't miss a thing that happens around here, baby sis. Believe that."

"How could you," Dexter queried, "with those Dumbo-size ears on the side of your head?"

Diamond laughed as Donald frowned. "Watch yourself," he said, his narrowed eyes fixed on Dexter. "Donovan's ears are shaped like mine."

"Dad, I'm not sure that is something I'd be pointing out," Diamond said, still laughing.

"Sister, it's something that he has no *need* to point out." Dexter's dark brown eyes twinkled and his brow wriggled as he looked pointedly at his father's ears and then at the replicas on his big brother.

Donald couldn't keep the frown on his face any longer. He burst out laughing. It had always been this way among his children: friendly teasing and healthy competition all held together with huge doses of love. From the beginning, he and his stay-at-home wife, Genevieve Drake, had raised their children to be a part of the business and had involved them in every aspect of their award-winning vineyard almost from the time they could walk. And while each person had their specific job title, theirs was a working knowledge of the business as a whole, and they were encouraged to multitask along those lines. This is how Diamond, the director of marketing and public relations, was now overseeing the major expansion project of turning Drake Vineyard into Drake Wines Resort & Spa.

Donovan was the most serious among the siblings, and no one was surprised when he steered the conversation back to business. "Do you believe the job will stay within the latest budget you've presented?"

"I'll have a better answer for you after I meet with the interior designer—" she looked at her watch "—which is happening very shortly. So if there are no more questions, gentlemen, I need to go."

A few minutes later, Diamond sat at her desk, speaking with her assistant before heading out of the office. "Kat, I'm going to the site to check out the construction, not the *candy*," she chided, though a smile belied Diamond's sternly delivered words. "Man candy" is what Kathleen Fitzpatrick had deemed the construction workers who'd invaded their space. For months, a crew of around fifty men had been hard at work building the five-star facility that upon completion would include restaurants, a bar, lounge, day spa, gym, expanded gift store, executive offices and boutique hotel.

"Besides," Diamond continued, "I'm not into candy right now. I'm watching my wait, spelled *W-A-I-T*." Kathleen fixed Diamond with a chagrined look. "I'm just not ready to jump back into the dating game." She reached for a batch of drawings and placed them in her briefcase. "And even if I were… there's no time for that. Duty continuously calls."

"Pretty good speech but that's hogwash and you know it." At fifty-six years old, Kathleen was not only Diamond's assistant, but sometimes she felt like a second mother to the woman who was twenty-plus years her junior. And after many years as a dedicated Drake employee, she felt comfortable speaking exactly what was on her mind. "It's been two years, girl. How long are you going to let that jerk of an ex-boyfriend run your life? Oh, my, did I say *run?* I meant *ruin!*"

"Ha! Stop exaggerating, Kat, before you set that Irish blood to boiling. My ex, whose name is no longer worthy of being uttered from my lips, has not ruined my life. He just helped to enhance my search skills and made me very selective. Right now, my man's first name is Resort and his last name is Spa."

"Go ahead. Hide behind your pesky professional obligations."

"You call a thirty-million-dollar renovation pesky? You go, girl!"

"But just remember," Kat continued, not missing a beat or taking the bait. "You're not getting any younger. You may have pushed it to the back of your mind, but I remember a young woman who not so long ago was eagerly looking forward to marriage and motherhood. The right man to make that happen is still out there."

"Amid the glass, bricks and plywood that currently litter our vineyard?"

"No, sweetie, perhaps amid the blood, sweat and mass of

muscles moving that stuff around! I'm not saying you should marry one of the workers, but you should at least take a look. I have and let me tell you…there's some honeys in the bunch."

Diamond's phone rang. It was just as well that the conversation end and that she take her mind off men—her sore spot—and put it back on work—her salvation. Besides, when it came to those particular M&Ms—men and marriage—there was no use arguing with her trusty assistant. Kathleen had wed at eighteen and borne five children. In her mind one hadn't lived until they'd snagged a man, had a child, adopted a dog and got a house surrounded by a white picket fence. She'd been married longer than Diamond had been alive. So when it came to heartbreak and breakups, what did she know?

"That was the designer," Diamond said after completing the call. "She's at the site. I'll be back in less than an hour."

The clicking of Diamond's four-inch heels punctuated the air as she walked to her parking space. She unlocked the door of her shiny sports coupe and slid inside. Belatedly realizing that the heat index in sunny Temecula, California, had risen, she shed her suit jacket, grabbed a pen in the cup holder and hastily placed her shoulder-length dark auburn hair into a chignon. The construction site was less than a mile away from Drake Wines' executive offices. As she drove down the picturesque lane lined with colorful maple trees boasting red, orange and yellow leaves in the autumn sun, Diamond knew her focus should be on windows, tiles and color swatches and making sure that every aspect of the job to which she'd been entrusted was being executed to perfection. Instead, it was on man candy.

# Chapter 2

Jackson "Boss" Wright leaned back in his large black executive chair with a satisfied smile. He and his team had done it again—outsmarted and outbid the big boys. Boss Construction had just won a lucrative contract for a downtown development in Chicago, Illinois. He couldn't wait to sit down with his team and fine-tune the plans, but first he needed to fly to Chicago for another meeting with the executives behind this combination shopping mall and office complex that would include a soaring edifice rivaling the Willis Tower. Jackson turned on his electronic calendar even as he reached for the speaker button on his office phone. At the same time, his office door opened and his assistant walked in. She was not smiling.

"We got another one," she said without preamble.

Jackson heaved a heavy sigh. Without asking, he knew what she meant. "Let me see it."

Marissa Hayes, Jackson's loyal assistant of six years, approached his desk, her outstretched hand containing a single sheet of paper. Jackson scanned it quickly. The note was short and succinct—as had been all the others.

*The bigger they are, the harder they fall. You think you've gotten pretty big, huh? Mr. Big-Time Construction, Mr. Millionaire Business Owner. Enjoy it while you can. Because your days at the top are numbered...just like the days of your life.*

Jackson casually tossed the piece of paper aside. He remained purposefully nonchalant, not wanting to upset Marissa more than this and the previous letters already had. "This is, what, the third or fourth one?"

"Fifth," Marissa somberly responded.

"Place it in the file with the others." Jackson scrolled the electronic calendar with his finger. "I need you to schedule meetings with all relevant parties of the Chicago project, including the mayor, if he's available. Then book a flight for the evening before."

"Returning when?"

"Either the evening of the last meeting or, if it's a dinner meeting, the next day's first flight." Jackson placed his iPad aside and walked over to a drafting table.

"So that's it?"

"What else is there? You already know to book me at the Ritz-Carlton Chicago, rent the car from—"

"Not the trip, Boss. I'm talking about the letter."

"What about it?"

"How long are you going to let these threats come before you do something about it?"

"What do you propose I do?"

Marissa worked hard not to let the exasperation she felt come out in her voice. "Call the police, hire an investigator, I don't know...but something!" So much for masking frustration. Even a blind man could have seen her chagrin.

Jackson noted the fear in Marissa's eyes. He didn't share it, but he didn't blame her. The first letter had arrived approximately two months ago, right after he'd ended a short-term affair. To say that the woman had been less than pleased was putting it mildly. She'd all but told him—in fact, she'd *actually* told him—that he'd regret the day he let her go. At first, he'd thought the letters were from her. But then again, it could be a former worker or subcontractor. He'd had to fire a few bad apples over the years. Maybe someone was still smarting from their termination—or being left off a job. He'd even considered the competition he'd beat out for the past few contracts. While the idea seemed highly unlikely, the construction business was a very competitive one. Boss Construction had landed several sweet deals in the past five years, outmaneuvering some pretty heavy hitters along the way. When billions of dollars were at stake and the national economy still shaky at best, who knew what companies were capable of? And finally there was Marissa's observation: that the letters began arriving shortly after he'd been featured in *Black Enterprise* magazine. The article, not to mention the accompanying photos, had resulted in a deluge of extra publicity—and fan mail. Maybe someone from his past had read it. Maybe someone from the life and the lifestyle he'd worked so hard to leave behind was trying to drag him back into it. But he wondered who would want to do that. And why? He'd left his old life more than a decade ago. Jackson wasn't so much concerned for himself as he was for those around him. For the first time, he fully acknowledged the potential extent of the threats. Damage could not only be done to him but to anyone in his offices. Marissa was right. It was time to take action.

"Call Abe," Jackson said, removing his jacket as he walked toward the walk-in closet at the back of the room. Abe Swartz was not only Jackson's attorney but a longtime friend. "Tell him we need a private investigator."

"Should I tell him why?" Marissa asked.

"Yes."

A moment later, Jackson stepped out of his office dressed in jeans, a T-shirt and work boots.

Marissa smiled as she eyed her supervisor's confident strides. She knew this routine. Jackson played the tough guy, and he was a typical alpha male. But he also had a huge heart, one that worried about those around him, those for whom he felt personally responsible. The anonymous threats were bothering him more than he let on. "Going to burn off some nervous energy?"

Jackson stopped at the outer office door, his hand on the knob. "Nervous? Do I look nervous? I'm going to engage in one of my favorite pastimes…working alongside my men."

## Chapter 3

*Man candy.* These were the words that came to mind as soon as she saw him. They'd exited a small building and now stood outside. *Who is he?* quickly followed that thought. As Diamond and the interior-design team had walked the floors of what would become the freestanding wine shop, she'd casually eyed the hardworking men. A couple she'd seen were buffed and toned, but others had average bodies and equally average looks. One or two had smiled and waved, but none had dared approach her. She'd smiled when she saw one worker nudge another after he'd surreptitiously winked at her. She figured her brothers had been their usually overprotective selves, warning the men to stay away from their little sister—no matter that she was the middle child or that said "little" sister stood five foot nine in stocking feet, with a full Beyoncé-like build and curves in all the right places. Growing up, she'd gone toe-to-toe with her brothers more than once, and until height and muscle replaced scraped knees and baby teeth, she'd pretty much held her own. Yet when it came to her and the opposite sex, the Drake line of defense was legendary. Every man she'd dated since the age of sixteen had come under intense and biased scrutiny. But she wasn't interested in dating.

*No interest. Too busy. I'm hardly even aware of these sweaty, shirtless, sexy men.* Or of the gorgeous man now eyeing her openly. Yeah. Right. And Mona Lisa was a man.

"Jackson Wright," Taylor said, when she noticed her last two sentences spoken to Diamond had gone unheard. There was a reason Taylor Stevens was one of the country's top interior designers. She had an uncanny eye for detail that missed nothing.

"I'm sorry?"

"The man you're totally aware of while trying hard to act as though you're not noticing him? His name is Jackson Wright."

Diamond tried for a quick recovery. "I don't know what you're talking about."

"If you mean you don't know about the stone foyer I was speaking of, you're right. Or the major design change I just mentioned. You haven't heard a word I've said. But don't worry. It's totally understandable. The first time I saw him my reaction was the same. But fair warning. I've heard that he's known for leaving women speechless and taking their breath away…among other things."

*Other things like what? Heart, soul, virginity?* Diamond did not voice these questions. She didn't want to appear interested in something that for her held absolutely no interest. Like human gods and whatnot. Diamond's appearances in and around the construction site had been rare. But one thing was for sure: she'd never seen this god, uh, guy before. He had a face—not to mention a body—that one would not forget.

She shifted her eyes away from the tall, commanding stranger. It was the only way she could refocus on the task at hand. *What is he...six-three, six-four?* She frowned, surprised that her thoughts had not shifted along with her body. So much for out of sight, out of mind. In less than two minutes, this man had gotten under her skin, and truth be told... Diamond wanted to get under him.

This surprised her. Diamond Nicole Drake was a strong, powerful woman, healthy enough but not normally given to forceful, almost primal, sexual urges. She knew how to focus; *discombobulated* would rarely if ever be used to describe her. As a high-powered executive in the multimillion-dollar dynasty her dad had created, she was a woman used to being in control and demanding respect. Well, she wanted to demand something, all right, and didn't care if it seemed the least bit disrespectful: a little rendezvous with Mr. Muscles. Private meeting. After hours. She'd even pay overtime.

*Get it together, sistah!* Why was she acting like she'd never seen a handsome man before? She had three of those in her immediate family. She'd grown up with fine men and dated them, too. Something about this construction worker unnerved her, and she wasn't exactly sure how she felt about it. What she did know for sure was that nothing was going to take her focus off of making Drake Wines the chic, upscale resort she'd envisioned. And speaking of visions, the one just over Taylor's shoulder was exactly what Diamond needed to bring her mind back to the singularly important task at hand—work.

With eyes still on the scene across what would become the resort courtyard, Diamond spoke to Taylor. "I'll be right back." Her long strides quickly ate up the distance between her and the group of men lounging on the ground. One was playing a video game, another two were checking out a sports magazine while a fourth was busy texting away. While still a couple yards away, she demanded, "What's going on here?" The men looked up, but before any of them could speak she looked at her watch and continued. "It's two o'clock in the afternoon, way past lunchtime. And you're reading magazines and playing video games?" She pushed her sunglasses from her face to the top of her head. "Really? Are you serious?"

"Diamond, we—"

"Do I know you?" Diamond asked the man who'd been texting on his cell phone. "Because in the workplace, unless otherwise specifically indicated, I am addressed as Ms. Drake."

Mr. *Sports Illustrated* tried next. "Ms. Drake, we—"

She held up her hand, deflecting further comment. "Never mind with the excuses. Where is your boss?"

Mr. Video Game pointed behind her. "He's right there."

Diamond turned, took one step and ran into a wall—otherwise known as the chest of Jackson Wright.

"Whoa!" Jackson reached out to steady a stumbling Diamond.

"Aw!" Diamond fell into Jackson's arms. *Is it me, or did the earth just quake?*

Later, Diamond would wonder about the tangible jolt of electricity that raced up her spine before coursing through her nether parts. But she gave no thought to that as she quickly put distance between herself and Jackson.

"Is there a problem?" Jackson asked, removing the large hand from around the soft arm he'd just steadied and crossing his arms over a massive chest.

"I'd say that's obvious," Diamond answered, crossing her arms, as well. "Your men are slacking on the job, and that is totally unacceptable."

"My men," Jackson began, his voice low and firm, "are on their lunch hour."

Diamond raised a skeptical brow. "At two in the afternoon?"

"That's right. We knew that Taylor would be conducting a walk-through and wanted to get to a certain point in the work before we stopped. And since these men will also be working past their usual cutoff time, this later lunch will help them get through what for some will be a twelve-hour day." Diamond's chin rose a notch as she continued to look at one of the most amazing examples of mankind she'd ever seen in life.

"They work very hard." Jackson's eyes narrowed as he awaited an answer—correction: an apology.

Diamond offered a different point of view. "How hard they've worked will be determined during the walk-through. And late lunch or not, playing video games and reading magazines on the job is not a good look."

"With all due respect, when on their lunch hour, my men can do whatever they want as long as it's legal."

When it came to the vineyard, it was a rare moment that someone challenged Diamond unless their last name was Drake. And when it came to nerve, Diamond realized that the man standing in front of her had plenty of it. And so did she, which was why he was going to get a serious piece of her mind. But realizing there was an avidly interested audience listening on, she decided now was not the time. Taking a deep, calming breath, she responded, "You may be over these men, but I am over this project. My name is—"

"I know who you are, Ms. Drake. And I also know California labor laws. That's part of my job." He extended his hand. "I'm Jackson Wright. The—"

"I know who you are," Diamond interrupted, paying him back for not letting her finish. She knew it was childish, unprofessional and something she'd probably not even do with her irksome brothers, but she seemed unable to stop this man from pushing her buttons. "You're the supervisor. Listen, I need to walk the site, but I'd like for you to call my assistant and set up a time to meet as soon as possible. There are some things we need to discuss."

Diamond started to walk around Jackson, but he fell into step beside her. "We'll make the appointment, but I'd actually like to handle the first part of the walk-through."

Diamond stopped. "Why?"

"To explain some of the technical aspects of the electrical installations, as well as share some thoughts I have for the restaurant and lounge atriums."

The last thing Diamond wanted was to spend additional time with Jackson Wright. His authoritative audacity intrigued her even as it irritated her. He had her thinking and feeling things she'd locked down deep.

And then fate intervened.

# Chapter 4

Taylor walked up to where Jackson and Diamond stood, her face a mask of worry as she talked into her cell. "Hold on," she said into the phone before looking at Diamond. "This is my assistant designer with a crazy emergency. Can you give me ten minutes to deal with this before we begin?"

"No problem," Jackson said, even though he hadn't been the one addressed. "I'll show Ms. Drake around."

Diamond was two seconds from going off on this presumptuous jerk, but her professional persona appeared unruffled. She turned to Taylor. "No worries, Taylor. Join us when you're done."

*She really doesn't know who I am.* This was Jackson's thought as they walked toward the second largest building in the new architectural scheme. For now, Jackson felt it unimportant to enlighten her. Strange things often happened when women found out he was the owner of Boss Construction: visions of wedding bells and baby booties often began to dance in their heads. Too bad he wasn't the marrying kind, because worse things could happen than having this feisty beauty in bed every night. But having her there for a night, a week, a few months even? It was a possibility, even with her head-strong personality. She was almost worth potentially losing a client over, but his uncle John had taught him nothing if not this one thing about business: don't play where you eat.

And then he went on flirting as if he'd never known Uncle John. "I've been involved in this project from the beginning, pretty lady, and would love to show you around. Let's start at the heart of the construction." Without waiting for an answer, he gently captured Diamond's elbow and steered her toward the large structure that when completed would be Temecula wine country's newest hotel. The restaurant, bar, lounge, gift store and retail offices would make up the ground floor.

Diamond ignored both the flirtatious comment and the shiver that ran down her spine at Jackson's touch. Instead, she lifted her chin and called on the age-old strength that was the Drake resolve: the power that had allowed her great-great-grandfather to not only participate in the Gold Rush but to become wealthy because of it; that had helped her great-grandfather stand his ground and keep hundreds of acres of land when those on both sides of the law tried to steal it from him; that had given her grandfather the foresight to turn many of those acres into top-quality, grape-producing vine-yards; and that had guided her father's vision into what was now the Drake dynasty—an immensely profitable, award-winning vineyard that was the envy of winemakers from Italy to France and Spain to Northern California. *He's just a man, flesh and blood. His presence is affecting me this way only because I'm sex-deprived,* Diamond thought, rationalizing the crazy attraction she was feeling for the man walking beside her. *That reality—not his good looks, bulging muscles or the way his butt fills out a pair of jeans—is why Jackson*

*Wright is affecting me so.* She shifted the purse that was over her left shoulder, deftly removing her skin from his touch.

Beside her, Jackson's thoughts followed a similar path... the one involving butts and bodies, that is. He marveled at the magnetism between them, thinking of how quickly he could palm the booty that had grabbed his attention as soon as Diamond had turned to speak with the designer. It was her perfectly curved derriere that had caused him to cut off his foreman in midsentence and make a beeline for the attractive woman across the way. Unfortunately, what he'd heard coming out of her mouth as she addressed the workers wasn't nearly as attractive as her round backside. But Jackson wasn't deterred. He could handle a strong woman because he was a strong man. And once he got her in bed, he determined, he'd show her a different kind of power altogether.

"Hold on, let me get you a hard-on, I mean, a hard hat. *Hat,*" he emphasized before quickly walking away. He walked toward a group of men huddled over a floor plan laid out on a truck hood. Diamond pondered how to deal with her uncanny attraction to someone she'd obviously be working with from here on out, even as she noticed how the men seemed to stand at attention as Jackson approached. They listened intently as he spoke with them. Then one of them reached into a crate and pulled out a hard hat. Jackson nodded his thanks and returned to Diamond's side.

"You seem to command a lot of respect," Diamond said as they continued walking toward the tall building. "Are you the supervisor or the foreman?"

"I'm in charge" was Jackson's noncommittal answer. "Put this on," he continued as they stepped inside the massive doorway and into a large, airy foyer.

"Is this really necessary? Most of the foundation and walks look almost complete."

"But they're not. Besides, everybody on-site wears a hard hat. That's the rule."

"You're not wearing one," Diamond responded sarcastically.

Jackson winked, blessing her with a smile. "I'm a rule breaker."

Diamond ignored the squiggle that went directly through her core in no time flat and refused to acknowledge the long, curly lashes that framed the dark brown eye that had winked at her, or the straight white teeth behind thick, cushy lips. She thought of those lips touching hers and used unresolved anger to push desire away. "We need to get something straight," she said, stopping as soon as they were out of sight of the men. "Don't ever question my word in front of your workers. And don't ever speak to me again in a tone of disrespect."

"Respect is earned," Jackson instantly retorted, rising up to his full six feet five inches. "And it's reciprocal. You respect me and my men, and we'll respect you."

"I beg your pardon?" Diamond was incredulous.

"You don't have to beg, Diamond. Just listen." His tone was so authoritative that she stopped talking in spite of herself. "The guys out there are men, not boys. This is work, not school. They were on their lunch hour, not recess. When they tried to explain this, you shut them up with a wave of your hand. Now, I don't know how you do it in the executive offices, but out here that's not how we get down." He stared at her without flinching, his eyes cool, unblinking.

Diamond stared back—and blinked first. "Perhaps I did jump to conclusions. But with the kind of money we're spending, we have the right to expect hard work and get it."

"You are getting what you're paying for," Jackson said, his tone softer as he once again touched Diamond's arm and guided her farther inside the structure. "And more. Come on in, and you'll see what I mean."

They walked through the foyer and into what would become the restaurant. "This is gorgeous," she gushed, shifting her eyes and thoughts from the brawn beside her to the beauty of the building, and once again removed her arm from his touch.

"Yes," Jackson replied, eyeing Diamond. "It is."

Diamond ignored the obvious come-on and stepped inside the main dining area. "The natural light from those large windows makes this space seem even bigger." Her tone was sharp, almost curt, and strictly business. "But they're going to allow in a lot of heat, as well. It gets very hot here in the summer, especially August and September. Even with stellar air-conditioning that might be a problem."

"These are special windows," Jackson explained, relaxing as he settled into his element. "They become tinted in extreme sunlight and temper the heat. Diners will still be able to take in the magnificent view yet not experience discomfort due to extreme heat or cold. The heating and cooling system that we've installed is state-of-the-art and will continually adjust to maintain whatever temperature is programmed into the computer. And these," Jackson continued, running his hands along the smooth, stone walls, "will also serve to both keep out the cold and…bring in the heat." Jackson made no move to hide his desire as his gaze openly raked Diamond's physique.

Diamond spun around, her chin lifting along with her ire. "Are you always this impertinent when speaking to a client? Or have you forgotten that that is who I am, a *client,* not some piece of meat to ogle like a rabid dog!"

*Bow wow wow, yippee yo, yippee yay, baby!* Her haughty nature turned him on, not off, and stimulated that part of him that liked a good challenge. He raised a brow as he stared back at her, noting how her ample chest heaved with her deep, calming breaths. He wanted to experience this spunkiness in a totally different way. Jackson's resolve to do so strengthened, even as his tactics changed. "I'm sorry. You're right. I'm out of line. But you're a very beautiful, desirable woman. I'd have to be blind not to find you attractive and dead not to react. It was just a little harmless flirtation, but again, I apologize."

"How harmless would it be if I reported you to the owner? I am here in a *professional* capacity, and I expect to be treated in a *professional* manner. Is that understood?"

"Completely," Jackson responded. Still, his eyes smoldered as he answered, and his wide-legged, crossed-arms stance suggested that he wasn't in the least bit afraid of being reprimanded. "Shall we continue, or would you prefer to do the tour with someone less intimidating?"

Diamond was not known for being a neck-rolling, hand-on-hip kind of sistah, but his comment almost provoked both actions. "What did you say?"

Throwing her off guard by changing courses yet again, Jackson reverted to a trait that more than once had saved his life—bravado. "You heard me. You're as attracted to me as I am to you. And that attraction, not my flirtation, is what's upsetting you."

"You have *got* to be kidding," Diamond countered, less angry with his insubordination than the fact that he'd hit the nail on the proverbial head. "Obviously someone has told you that you're God's gift to women…and you believed them."

Jackson's grin was cocky yet genuine. "I've been considered a present a time or two."

"Well, the only thing that's a wrap right now is this conversation. You might want to brush off your résumé because after I have a little chat with the owner you'll probably be unemployed." Diamond turned and headed for the door.

"Wait," Jackson said, reaching out and stopping her. She looked down at the hand squeezing her arm and up into pleading eyes. "Please," he continued, releasing her, while imagining the confusion and laughter that would ensue among his men if she went out there demanding to speak to the owner. "I promise to behave." Now it was Diamond's turn to cross her arms. Her look showed that she didn't believe him. "I need this job," he finished.

"Then you need to climb out of your Neanderthal cave and realize that the days of women's butts being patted in the workplace and sexual innuendo being the standard are long gone."

"Got it."

"I hope you do. Because one more ill-mannered remark and you're history."

"I'll be the perfect gentleman from here on out."

"See that you do." With that, Diamond turned and headed back through what would eventually be the dining room and into the future top-of-the-line kitchen. Jackson answered her questions, professionally and knowledgeably, showing a strong command of the entire project as they moved from the restaurant to the gift shop, then down the hall to the retail offices. Finally, they crossed the lobby and entered the lounge that was situated across from the restaurant. They crossed the Plexiglas-covered dance floor, part of which would house an aquarium, to an expansive DJ booth—one of the few parts of the room that looked completed. Diamond walked up to a large control board. "What's all this?" she asked.

"Magic," Jackson simply replied. "This system allows the controller to create whatever atmosphere that's desired, whether its disco, blue light in the basement, rave, holiday."

Diamond lightly ran her hands over the knobs. "Looks complicated."

"It is." Jackson closed the distance between them. "May I?" he asked, stepping up to the controls and directly beside

Diamond. She nodded and took a step away from him. "I was a DJ back in my college days. And a bit of a geek."

Diamond said nothing, although she thought that "geek" and "Jackson" in the same sentence sounded like bad English.

"This controls the lighting," he began, his voice the epitome of expertise. "See how it goes from bright to dim? And we can also adjust the colors, bounce them off the walls, ceiling, floors or a combination of the three." Diamond watched as Jackson's large, tapered fingers deftly moved from one button to the next. "There are currently eight thousand songs programmed into this computer," he continued, taking a step toward Diamond to punch a button in front of her. "Check this out." Jackson leaned forward and unconsciously placed a hand on her waist. "I'm sorry," he said, quickly removing it. Diamond immediately missed his touch. He turned on a computer, entered a few commands, and within seconds a list of music genres filled the screen. "The sound system is incredible. What type of music do you like?"

"All kinds," Diamond replied. Jackson clicked on a link and began scrolling through songs. "Especially upbeat," she quickly added. The lights were dim, and the last thing Diamond needed was a love song to conjure up images of a certain male body, sans clothing, hard and ready for love.

Jackson flashed a knowing smile. He clicked on an album cover, and soon the sounds of music filled the room. Jackson played with the controls and psychedelic colors bounced off the walls. He flipped another switch, and smoke began swirling down from the ceiling.

"Wow!" Diamond said as she looked at the magic Jackson had spoken of and imagined the room packed with happy dancers. She smiled as Jackson bobbed his head and sang in tune to a popular song. Watching the way he moved his hips to the beat, Diamond could well imagine just how exciting it would be to spend a night with him. *Would be? Girl, what in the heck are you thinking?* There would absolutely, positively be no woulda, shoulda, coulda with this hunkalicious guy standing beside her. Diamond well knew his kind: cocky and arrogant, probably certain that he could get her into his bed. She was certain of that, too, but that was beside the point. Fortunately, she had an iron-clad rule to save her from herself. She never, ever dated anyone in or near the workplace. After a two-month courtship with a former sales manager had ended in a stalker situation with law enforcement involved, she'd vowed to keep her personal and professional lives very separate.

"Now watch how the DJ has the ability to completely change the mood." Once again, Jackson clicked on the song list. The sounds of a sultry saxophone filled the room, the smooth jazz tune evoking images of lovemaking more than words ever could.

Diamond was convinced she was losing it. How else could she explain the fact that she was now undressing Jackson with her eyes? It was a good thing that his back was to her as he continued to fiddle with the knobs—a good thing because it gave her several uninterrupted seconds to take in his broad shoulders, strong back, narrow waist, perfect butt, strong thighs, long legs and big feet. As she continued to stare at his perfect backside encased in jeans, Diamond could barely remember her name.

She looked up in time to see the room darken; tiny lights resembling twinkling stars filled the ceiling. The air in the room shifted along with the lighting. Diamond felt it and believed that Jackson did, too. Attraction crackled like a burning log between them. And what happened to the air in the room? He turned and looked at her, his gaze penetrating, yet unreadable. Diamond forced herself not to look away, tried to maintain the stare, but again…she couldn't. Her eyes dropped to those delectable lips that sat under an aquiline nose, just as

Jackson flicked out his tongue to moisten them. The sax sizzled from the speakers, wrapping them in a sensual cocoon, a world of their own. It was as if time stopped, along with Diamond's rational thinking. Because for the life of her she couldn't think of anything more logical to do than to kiss those lips, to crush the nipples that were even now hardening at the mere thought of being touched against Jackson's hard chest.

She took a step.

Jackson's eyes narrowed as he watched her come closer. He looked at her lips, slightly parted with desire. Wanting him was written all over her face. His message was being proclaimed from an area decidedly lower, by a rapidly increasing bulge in the front of his jeans.

He took a step.

They now stood just inches apart, neither moving, barely breathing. At the risk of having to fire himself for insubordination, Jackson reached out and ran a finger along Diamond's jawline. His touch was more electric than the guitar that now accompanied the sax. She licked her lips and suppressed a shiver. He watched, wondering how they tasted, those lips, wanting to know how she tasted. Her eyes flickered shut and then back open, even as her head tilted seemingly of its own accord. To hell with stalking ex-coworkers and iron-clad declarations. She would be a rule breaker, too. Thoughts of consequences could come later. Right now all she wanted were his lips...on hers...now! He bent his head down. One more step and the kiss would begin. Just one more step...

"There you are!" Taylor said as she entered the room. And right behind her? Donald and Donovan: father and son.

*Damn!*

Diamond scurried from the intimacy of the DJ booth and Jackson's captivating eyes, looking as professional as she could with her body on fire. She ignored Donald's scowl and

Donovan's smirk and tried to remember how to construct a sentence. *Subject, verb, noun, Diamond. Subject! Verb! Noun!*

Jackson came to her rescue, and in the moment, had he rode in on a white horse, dressed in armor, she couldn't have been any more grateful. "Mr. Drake, always a pleasure to see you, sir. Donovan, good to see you, man." They shook hands.

"Good to see you," Donovan replied, his brow creased in slight confusion.

Jackson knew that further talk with these two men would likely blow his cover. It was time for a quick getaway. "Ms. Drake, it's been a pleasure," he said, his tone courteous, formal, making Diamond immediately wish for the rogue. "But I need to head over to the other building. Gentlemen, if you'll excuse me."

Forcing herself not to watch the firm, hard butt exiting the building, Diamond turned to her dad and brother. "What are you guys doing here?"

"We were on our way to the cellar and saw Taylor outside. When she said you were here, on the first floor of our masterpiece, we thought we'd join you."

"Good, because so far what I've seen is amazing." Jackson's leaving allowed oxygen to once again flow to Diamond's brain. "Taylor, why don't you explain to Dad and Donovan what you shared with me earlier, including the fabrics and colors for the spa?" They continued the tour, and Taylor presented a variety of swatches. But in her mind, the only hue Diamond saw was caramel, and the only face was that of Jackson Wright.

## Chapter 5

A half hour later, Diamond wheeled her shiny black BMW into its parking space, threw the car in Park and shut off the engine. She hadn't seen him when they left the site but no matter. Thoughts of Jackson still consumed her. She'd never had her head spun like this, not even when Jamal Pendergrass had kissed her outside the skating rink—her first smooch at the ripe old age of thirteen. What just happened? Diamond didn't understand. As a woman who prided herself on self-control and was known in the dating world as being "hard to get," she was less than enthused that she'd almost made a fool of herself in the workplace. As it was, when she saw her father, in general, and Donovan, in particular, she knew she'd have some 'splainin' to do! Her older brother's knowing smirk hadn't gone unnoticed.

Determined to put Jackson and what had happened behind her, she took a deep breath, reached for her purse and headed into the executive offices. She pasted what she hoped was a nonchalant look on her face, took another calming breath—where was the yoga mat when she needed it?—and opened the door to her office.

Kathleen looked at her always cool, calm and collected superior and immediately sensed something amiss. "What's wrong?"

"Does it look like something's wrong with me?" Diamond snapped. So much for the calm, nonchalant facade.

"You forget how well I know you," Kathleen replied, nonplussed. "Plus, I know a tight mouth when I see one. Come on, darlin'. Out with it. Did one of those pieces of man candy get you all hot and bothered?"

Diamond didn't respond.

Kathleen clapped her hands with glee. "That's it! Which one? No, don't tell me, let me guess. Is it that tall, strapping man with the tattoo across his chest?"

The "tall, strapping" description definitely fit Jackson, but Diamond didn't remember a tattoo. "Step into my office," she said over her shoulder to Kathleen as she left the common area to enter her more private domain. Maybe talking about this weird attraction would help her get rid of it.

Kathleen hurried behind her, closing Diamond's office door once they were both inside. Her green eyes glittered as she took a seat in one of the tan suede chairs that framed the large ebony desk. Diamond walked behind it, threw down her purse and slouched into the large leather executive chair.

"First of all, nothing is wrong. And, for the record, you're right. There are a lot of attractive men down there."

"Anyone in particular catch your fancy?"

Diamond shrugged. "Not really." *Liar, liar, pants on fire.* "I was given a partial tour by the supervisor while Taylor handled a call."

"And…"

"And nothing, Kat. Jeez! He's tall, but then so are several

of the men. Plus, he was wearing a T-shirt." Much to her chagrin. "I don't remember a tattoo."

"The one I'm talking about stands a head and shoulder above the rest. He's a hunk of burning love," Kathleen said dreamily. "I don't see him every day, but the few times I have, he's left quite an impression. Oh, to be young and single again. I bet his legs aren't the only things that are long and strong about him."

"Kathleen!"

"Oh, come now," Kathleen said, her eyes still twinkling. "You don't think I became a mother of five by singing 'Yankee Doodle,' do you?"

"Ha! I guess not. The man who showed me around is really tall."

"Handsome?"

"He looks all right. His name is Jackson."

"Dear, you're trying really hard not to sound impressed, which means he must have knocked your socks off." Kathleen leaned forward. "So when are you guys going out?"

"Out?"

Kathleen clucked. "Out…as in on a date? Really, Diamond, sometimes I wonder if you're twenty-nine or only nine."

"We're not going out," Diamond responded, ignoring the older woman's jab. "I don't date men from the workplace."

"He's hardly that," Kathleen insisted. "He doesn't work for Drake Wines, and he's not in these offices. I think you should go out with him," she went on, despite Diamond's scowl. "If nothing else, it will rid you of the persnickety mood you've had of late. You know I love you, Diamond, but in the past few months, you haven't been your charming, gracious self."

"Careful, Kat," Diamond drily replied, turning on her computer and reaching for the mouse. "You're talking to the woman who signs your paychecks."

"Technically, my paychecks are signed by your father and

the CFO. But you're the boss, so I'll button my lip and head back to my desk." Kathleen reached the door and turned. "But I still think you should go out with him. Who knows what that might lead to?" Her tinkling laughter followed her out of the room.

Diamond couldn't help smiling as she clicked on her task bar and checked out what was left on the day's agenda. Kathleen was Diamond's assistant, but having worked in various capacities at the vineyard for twenty years, she was family, too. *She's right,* Diamond acknowledged, as she scrolled down the page. *I haven't been too charming lately.*

And Diamond knew why. It was the lack of testosterone in her life and, more specifically, in her bed—a problem she didn't see being resolved anytime soon. Even as she shifted from her task bar to her calendar and the evening's obligation—a fundraiser for at-risk youth sponsored by the San Diego Arts Association—she pondered her predicament and Kathleen's earlier comment. How long was she going to let Benjamin Carter, the ex-fiancé who'd strung her along before breaking her heart, ruin her life?

Abruptly cutting off her computer, Diamond reached for her purse and strode toward the door. Kathleen was right. Benjamin's refusal to marry her after their long engagement had affected her more than she dared admit. She had buried herself in work and put her life on hold because of it. She'd gone on only a couple dates in almost a year and was probably setting herself up to be an old maid. *But no more!* "It's time to get back in the game!" she hissed. Maybe she'd meet someone tonight to play with.

Moments later, Diamond had lowered the top of her convertible and was zooming down the tree-lined roads of Drake Vineyard, soon to be known as Drake Wines Resort & Spa. As she neared the construction site, Jackson's handsome face and knowing smile drifted into her mind. She remembered the feel of his hand on her waist, and her body reacted, muscles in certain nether regions clenching at the mere possibility of surrounding someone else's, well, muscle. In spite of her determination not to do so, she eased off the gas, slowing down as her eyes scanned the sweaty bodies still hard at work under the dimming sun. She didn't see him. She told herself that was a good thing and realized that lying to oneself was not cute.

Diamond reached for her phone and called her hair stylist, who was located in San Diego. "Lecia, it's Diamond."

"And let me guess," Lecia said, as she sewed a track of hair into the head of her current client. "You need to see me ASAP, and I'm supposed to fit you in."

Diamond laughed. "Something like that. But it's an emergency. I need a makeover."

"Oh, Lord. Sounds serious. What time can you be here?"

"In about an hour, hour and a half?"

"You'd better be glad I consider you a friend."

"Plus I tip well."

"Ha! That, too. Which I appreciate, since some of these fools hand me an extra dollar and call it a day."

"You hook me up, and I'll make it worth your while. See you soon." Diamond ended the call and was soon speeding down the boulevard to the estate where the entire Drake family still lived. Initially, she'd not been looking forward to a night of gowns and tuxes and rich men trying to impress her with their portfolios. But a certain assistant had suggested change, and a certain well-built construction worker had whetted her appetite. Before the night was over, she decided, she'd find someone to get back in the game with, and try to forget about the man with whom she'd really like to score.

# Chapter 6

Jackson pulled up to the valet and exited his latest toy. Next to women, cars were one of his favorite things to collect, and the newly purchased top-of-the-line Maserati GranTurismo fit him to a T. Like him, it was sleek, powerful and stood out in a crowd. He unfolded his tuxedo-clad six-foot-five-inch frame from the sports car, cutting a distinctive swath across the five-star hotel's well-appointed lobby. Envious glances and flirty stares followed him as he walked to the meticulously landscaped garden, where gloved waiters carried trays of bubbly and hors d'oeuvres. Taking a flute from a passing waiter, he surveyed the grounds quickly filling up with the beautiful people: silk, diamonds, cloying perfume and smiles abounding. For a fleeting second the boy he used to be—poor, insecure, troubled—rose up within him. He wondered how these people would react if they knew where he'd grown up, the things he'd done to survive that childhood and where his mother now resided. A beautiful woman coming toward him distracted him from these uncomfortable thoughts. By the time she arrived at his side, the bravado Jackson had often called upon to mask his fears was firmly back in place.

"Jackson, thanks for accepting my invitation." Her sparkling blue eyes drank him in much faster than he sipped his champagne. "You look delicious. I'm so glad you came." She reached up and planted a soft kiss on his chin. "And unaccompanied no less," she whispered seductively. "A virile man such as yourself shouldn't spend the night alone."

Jackson smiled at Erin Bridges, the daughter of a real-estate mogul with whom Jackson had partnered on occasion. No one could deny her classic beauty: shiny blond hair cut into a flattering asymmetrical bob, bright doe eyes framed by ridiculously long lashes and a pouty mouth covered with just the right amount of shimmering gloss. She'd definitely caught his eye when they met five years ago, but after realizing that the business relationship with her father would be an ongoing one with lucrative potential, Jackson had decided that they should not date. Again, his uncle's warning to not use his workplace as a playground helped him put on the brakes. She'd been less than happy with his "let's just be friends" suggestion. But what could she do?

"I see you've pulled off yet another top-notch event," Jackson finally said, waving his hand in acknowledgment of the well-heeled crowd.

"It's easy to do when you have friends in high places," Erin responded. "Besides, this cause really feels good. With the fundraisers planned, we'll be able to send at least twenty-five students to highly accredited colleges and, after graduation, through our partnerships with local businesses such as yours, help some of them get started in their professional careers. Oh, speaking of local businesses, someone has just come in that I want you to meet."

Jackson turned to see to whom Erin referred and saw a

vision that took his breath away. Diamond Drake lived up
to her name, lighting up the courtyard as she waltzed in,
the epitome of grace and beauty. Her dress was a simple
one-shoulder design, the deep-red iridescent fabric perfectly
complementing her sun-kissed sienna skin. Jackson's eyes
continued to travel upward, taking in a long neck and what?
*She cut her hair!* The short hairdo fit her spunky personality, he immediately decided, noting that it emphasized her
high cheekbones and almond-shaped eyes. Her makeup was
simple, as was her jewelry. *When you are a diamond, you
don't need to overaccessorize.* His gait was strong and purposeful, his thoughts predatory, as he walked toward her.

Later, Diamond would pride herself on not having tripped
in her four-inch heels as shock consumed her. *What is he
doing here?* This was a five-thousand-dollar-per-person
gathering of the county's most elite players. How did a construction worker, even a foreman, wrangle an invite and then
afford such an expensive one? And how did one transform
from looking perfectly at home on a construction site, complete with sweaty T-shirt and dusty jeans, to looking as if he
owned the world in a tux that emphasized his broad shoulders, narrow waist and long legs, and a stark white shirt that
highlighted caramel skin? Diamond's eyes narrowed as they
finally settled on the woman walking beside Jackson, La
Jolla's premiere socialite, Erin Bridges. She felt as if she were
looking at the answer to how Jackson got invited to the event
and didn't try and ignore the stab of jealousy that arose at
the prospect that the construction site might not be the only
place Jackson was making use of his skilled hands.

"Diamond, you look lovely!" Erin reached Diamond with
arms outstretched and gave air kisses to both cheeks. "You
cut your hair. I love it!"

"Decided it was time for a change," Diamond said, running

a hand through the shortened crop she was still getting used to, and feeling suddenly shy under Jackson's intense gaze. With effort, she kept her eyes on Erin. "You look amazing. That dress is stunning."

"Oh, just a little something I picked up last week in Italy. It's a Roberto Cavalli original."

"Roberto...of course." Diamond's statement was to Erin, but she'd lost the fight to keep her eyes off Jackson. Or was his name Magnet? By the way she was drawn to him, she couldn't tell.

"Diamond, I'd like you to meet Jackson Wright, the 'Boss' of Boss Construction and philanthropist to a variety of worthwhile causes."

Diamond's eyes narrowed as realization dawned. Her father and brothers had always referred to the owner of the construction company as Boss, not Jackson. Diamond had assumed they were simply referring to him by his title and had never considered that the name of the company actually referred to a person. It had never mattered to her one way or the other—until now. "So...is your name Jackson or Boss?"

"Jackson, but most of my friends call me Boss."

"Making sure that everyone knows you're the head honcho?"

"That's what my mom called me. She said that even in diapers I was pretty headstrong and was barking orders by the time I was crawling. The nickname stuck." It was one of the few things from his childhood that Jackson had kept.

Diamond felt enough sparks were flying to send a shuttle to the moon. She stared at Jackson and barely noticed when a guest came over to steal Erin away. For a moment, she lost herself in the heat emanating from Jackson's gaze and wondered how hot his kiss would feel. Diamond let the fire in her core rise to her brain. Earlier, Jackson had duped her. He hadn't come clean about who he was at the job.

"Boss Wright?" she murmured, her face fixed in a look of subtle chagrin. "*Owner* of Boss Construction?" She realized that Jackson was still holding her hand and deftly pulled it away from him.

"At your service," Jackson replied, nonplussed, reaching to grab her hand again.

"Stop it!" Diamond spat between clenched teeth, even as she worked to maintain a neutral expression for anyone watching. "You've got a lot of nerve standing here all nonchalant after lying to me this afternoon."

"Lying? How so?"

"By not telling me who you were when showing me around the construction site."

"Oh, you mean back at the vineyard where you were acting like a spoiled BAP, the Black American princess threatening to have me fired because I came on to you? I didn't lie to you. There were simply some things that I didn't reveal."

Diamond cursed her body for reacting to this silkily drawled truth. "I specifically spoke about discussing you with the owner."

"Which you may have known were one and the same had you not interrupted my introduction. Assuming that I was the supervisor is on you."

"I'd say you were being uncooperative at best and deceptive at worst."

"Well, baby," Jackson said, the single glass of bubbly obscuring his common sense, the intense desire for her usurping the lack of confidence left over from his early years and pride developed in his later ones, "you're getting ready to have a cause for rank insubordination because I've got to be honest. Before this night is over, I'd like to get real acquainted with those soft, luscious-looking lips of yours and find out if the rest of your body is as soft as your arm. How's that sound?"

"It sounds like a man who'd like to get slapped," Diamond

retorted, even as the image she'd fought all afternoon—the one that had them skin to skin from head to toe—flashed in her mind. "It sounds like a cocky, arrogant jerk who has obviously gotten women to drop their panties way too easily."

"Well, there is some truth to that."

"I think I've heard enough."

She got ready to walk away, but Jackson's words stopped her. "Ask yourself why I'm so getting on your nerves, why you've been snapping at me since we've met. And don't feed yourself the lame excuse that it's because of not knowing who I was at the site."

"Well, you should know about lame."

"Wow, spoken like a princess reprimanding the help." He continued despite her huff. "Maybe I should have come clean and told you I owned the company, but I'm glad I didn't. My anonymity gave me the opportunity to see firsthand how you treat my men. And like I said this afternoon, you don't have the right to talk down to them or anyone else."

*Did this fool just check me on how I handle my business on my property?* "I'll admit that your men have always been respectful, an area in which you could learn a thing or two. Like now, telling me how to act and what to say. Just who do you think you are?"

"A man who's not afraid of your last name, that's who," Jackson replied. Mr. Bravado was obviously still riding shotgun. "And one who sees what he wants and goes after it." Diamond got ready to interrupt him, but Jackson held up his hand and continued. "You've got quite the reputation among the men—powerful, no nonsense, untouchable. They say you don't come to the site much, and when you do, you keep your distance. But I detect a fire underneath that cool exterior. We're grown folk, Diamond, and I have no need to beat around the bush. I find you attractive as hell, and I want to get to know you better…a lot better. I think you want to get to know me, too. Am I right?"

Diamond's chin took on its familiar tilt as she tried not to let Jackson's words affect her. The fact of the matter was she was feeling him in more ways than one and not only that but she wanted him to feel her in more ways than one. He was a handsome, intelligent man who she'd bet her paycheck was an awesome lover. But after he'd sexed her real good, then what? And what about her rule of not dating within the workplace, not to mention the one about not having any more casual relationships with noncommittal men? If there was one thing Diamond could spot, it was a man with marital allergies. Her brothers Donovan and Dexter had shown her exactly what that looked like.

As if on cue, said brothers walked into the space and up to where she and Jackson were standing. A part of her was glad to see them as they'd provided an escape of sorts. But the other part knew that her reprieve was over. She'd avoided both her father and Donovan this afternoon, but she was in for a grilling later on tonight. "Hey, bro," she said, reaching up to give Dexter a hug. "I didn't think you were going to make it."

"I just got in," Dexter responded, eyeing Jackson as he gave his sister a hug.

"How was Baltimore?"

"Cool. Rainy." Dexter took a step back. "Why are you so dressed up? And what happened to your hair?"

"Dressing up is normally required at a black-tie event," Diamond sarcastically answered. She fingered her hair. "Do you like it?"

"Yeah, it looks good." Dexter held up his fist to Jackson for a pound. "Hey, Boss."

"Dexter," Jackson responded, before turning to greet Donovan, as well. "Hey, Don. This is why I had to cut our meeting short, man. If I'd known you were coming here, I would have let you know."

"Looks like there's a few things I might need to know," Donovan replied, before turning to Diamond. "I didn't know you and Diamond were hanging out."

"Just formally met her today, man. And now I see why y'all have been keeping her under wraps!"

"Yes, just how has that happened?" Diamond asked Donovan. "How is it that you, Dex and Dad have known Jackson 'Boss' Wright for a while now and I'd never met him before today?"

"No need," Donovan said with a shrug. "You'd never been a part of the construction projects before, and most of our initial meetings took place at Boss's office." What Donovan didn't share was that it was also to protect his baby sis from getting hurt. He knew that Diamond wanted to get married and knew that Jackson was a Casanova. Like oil and water— those two ingredients didn't mix well. "Don't let the smooth talk fool you, baby sis. This is a great businessman, but he doesn't let the grass grow under his feet...if you know what I mean."

"Don't worry, Donovan. Our interaction is strictly business."

Jackson chuckled but instead of responding to Diamond's comment, still smiling, he addressed Donovan instead. "You're being a bit hard on a brother, don't you think?"

"Just keeping it real," Donovan replied, his gruff words tempered by a smile of his own.

"Should Diamond grant me the pleasure of her extended company, I'll be the perfect gentleman."

Donovan eyed Jackson skeptically, even as he nodded at Erin, who was motioning for him from across the lawn to join the group she now entertained. "You do that," he said, giving the construction owner a fist pound and then leaving the group.

Dexter smiled as a gorgeous Latina sidled up to him. "Hey, Maria," he said, giving her a light kiss on the lips. "I think I'll freshen up my drink and then we'll take our seats. The concert is about to begin."

"Shall we join them?" Jackson asked Diamond.

Diamond thought about sitting next to Jackson while listening to the sultry sounds of smooth jazz, feeling the breeze from the ocean and experiencing the accidental brushes of his fingers across her flaming skin. Not a good idea. "Thanks but I think I'll network a bit more. Oh, and Jackson, I meant what I said to my brother. The interaction between us is to be strictly business. Have I made myself clear?"

Jackson slowly nodded. "Got it." He stood there watching and appreciating her "business" as she walked across the lawn to join her friends.

*Chapter 7*

Diamond shifted in her seat, hoping that she didn't look as unnerved as she felt. For the past thirty minutes, she could have sworn that she'd felt the heat of Jackson's gaze on the nape of her neck. She'd known the moment he sat down directly behind her not because the woman next to him had immediately introduced herself and her husband but because there was a vibe, an energy, between them that alerted Diamond to whenever he was within touching distance. With every note that oozed from Paul Taylor's saxophone, Diamond felt the heat in her body rise. She watched Paul's nimble fingers as he keyed the melodious notes, but in her mind, Jackson's hands were on her body, playing a song written for her alone.

"Do you want a drink?" Diamond asked her brother, right in the middle of Taylor's solo.

Donovan looked at her questioningly. "You're getting one right now?" he whispered.

Diamond nodded as she composed herself.

"I'll have a beer."

"I'll be right back."

She eased into the aisle and headed to the bar. Taking deep breaths, she willed her heart to stop its erratic pounding and for her body to behave. Before reaching the bar, she decided to take a quick stroll around the gardens, regain her poise, get the drinks and then take her seat once the song ended. The sun had set, and the night sky had come alive with thousands of stars surrounding a bright, full moon. Lamps were strategically placed throughout the garden, highlighting the various shrubs, flowers and other greenery. Diamond took the path nearest the bar and headed toward a fountain near the end of the garden's east side.

Just before she got there, a hand reached out and grabbed her.

Diamond gasped, and in that moment, a tongue on a mission slipped into her open mouth. A strong arm wrapped itself around her waist, and another hand massaged the nape of her neck. The woodsy smell of Jackson's cologne engulfed her, and even though her mind was telling her to pull back, slap his face and curse him out, her traitorous body was pressing against his, even as her tongue engaged in a languid duel. Before she knew what was happening, her arms had reached around to stroke his broad back, and she marveled at the power created by sinew and bone. Somewhere in her mind she felt one of his hands muss up her short do. Jackson moaned and deepened the kiss. His other hand traveled from her shoulder to the small of her back and lower still until it cupped her round, firm booty as if the most natural thing in the world to be doing on a night like this was to be ravished in a moonlit garden while jazz played in the background.

Jackson slowly raised his head and blazed a trail of kisses from her mouth to her neck and back to her temple. "I said

I'd be a gentleman," he whispered, even as he nipped her earlobe with tiny love bites, "so I should have asked to kiss you. But an apology at this point would be insincere. You taste way too good for me to feel sorry for what just happened." Jackson ran a firm finger down Diamond's arm. "May I kiss you again?" he asked. His voice was as soft as the kisses he'd rained down on her face. Her nod was almost imperceptible, but her acquiescence was all Jackson needed to raise the stakes. He pulled them deeper into the shadows, backed her against the ivy-covered brick wall and once again plundered her mouth with his tongue. His hips mirrored the movement of his tongue: slow, rhythmic circles as he thrust up against her.

Diamond wasn't even aware that she was joining in the dance of this slow grind until she felt Jackson harden beneath her. Then she felt his hand on the silk of her dress, grasping her hip, easing along her waist and up to her breast. He tweaked her nipple, and Diamond felt as if she would explode. In this love-induced insanity, it didn't matter that she was in a public place, mere yards from where her protective brothers sat. All she wanted was this man's arms around her, with his body pressed tight against hers.

And then the audience applauded.

"Stop!" Diamond used the last ounce of her will and pushed against Jackson's massive chest. "We…can't do this."

"I know," Jackson readily agreed. "You're much more than a quick romp in the hay or, in this instance, the garden. Here," he said as he reached inside his jacket pocket and pulled out a card. "My cell number is on the back. Call me. Let's meet up and…finish what we've started." In the next instant, he was gone.

Diamond stayed behind in the shadows, willing her heartbeat to return to normal. She touched a hand to her lips and felt them swollen from the passion of his kisses. She felt that one look at her brothers and the message of what had transpired would be sent faster than a cell phone text. She'd been ravished by Jackson Wright, and she wanted it to happen again and again. Diamond knew it would raise eyebrows and questions, but she had no choice. She couldn't get Donovan's drink, return to her seat, hear the rest of the concert or say thanks to the host. If she was going to save any dignity at all, she had to run out of here as if the devil were chasing her. And that is exactly what she did.

## Chapter 8

Diamond stood in her bedroom, ready to greet the day. This had always been one of her favorite rooms in the house, with its separate sitting area and massive bath. On her eighteenth birthday, she'd changed the color scheme from girly pinks and purples to a dramatic black-and-white theme. Just last year she'd changed it again. Now rich tan-colored walls and plush ivory bedding, both of which complemented the dark walnut floors, gave the room a sophisticated yet understated elegance. Splashes of color came courtesy of recently purchased Charles Bibbs artwork and freshly cut flowers that always occupied the coffee table and fireplace mantel. At times she thought about venturing out and purchasing a condo or house of her own. But then she'd come to this, her retreat, and forget every thought she had about leaving.

Diamond took one last look in the mirror. She looked calm and refreshed, thanks to a two-hour early-morning workout. This fresh look covered the roiling emotions she felt from her encounter with Jackson two days ago. For this she was thankful, since she was getting ready to walk downstairs and join her family for their traditional Sunday dinner. Everyone would be there, and she was sure all eyes would be on her. Why did she know this? Because she knew how her family operated, and there was very little that happened with one Drake that the others didn't know about sooner or later. Donovan was very close to their father, Donald, so Diamond was sure he'd mentioned her encounter with Jackson and her refusal to discuss it when asked. Dexter was the baby of the family and a mama's boy. Additionally, he couldn't hold water if he carried it in a bucket—an old-time saying that meant he couldn't keep a shred of anybody else's business to himself. Knowing this, Diamond had basically avoided her parents for two days, which—even though she and Dexter still lived at home—wasn't hard to do. The estate included a main house and three fully equipped guest rooms totaling ten thousand square feet. Each child had their own wing, as did their parents. More often than not, Donovan could be found there, too, even though he'd purchased a home near San Diego a few years ago. Diamond's grandparents, David and Mary Drake, lived in one of the guest homes. Their ninety-eight-year-old great-grandfather still lived on the property, as well. These were the people Diamond saw as she rounded the corner and entered the dining room.

"Well, the princess finally decided to grace us with her presence. How are you, baby girl?" Donald Drake came around the table and hugged his daughter. A commanding presence at six foot two and two hundred pounds, Donald had taken the business from a successful company to a dynasty when he'd expanded Drake Wines into most of the fifty states and then internationally. He'd also been on the cutting edge of the health-conscious craze. Their vineyard had gone organic many years ago.

"Good afternoon, Dad." Diamond gave Donald a hug. "Hello, Mom. I love it when you cook for us. Dinner smells great!"

"Ha! It's your grandparents who have the chef, dear. I've cooked dinner almost every Sunday since you were born. But thank you."

After hugging her mom, Genevieve, Diamond greeted everyone else in the room. "Sorry I'm just now coming down. I didn't know y'all were waiting on me."

"Your timing is perfect, dear," Genevieve replied, looking as gracious as ever with her long silver hair swept up in a loose bun. A little dynamo, who at all of five foot five ruled the roost, she was also one of the most loving people on the planet. "Your father's just giving you a hard time."

The family shared small talk as they dished up the succulent feast: roasted duck with fresh vegetables—corn, greens, squash, carrots and onions—from Grandma Mary's large and flourishing garden, juicy heirloom tomatoes, garlic mashed potatoes seasoned with Genevieve's fresh grown herbs, Mary's spicy corn bread and, of course, a fruity pinot noir from the Drake vineyards. After the patriarch, Great-grandfather David Drake Sr.—affectionately referred to as Papa Dee—blessed the food, everyone dug in.

"Dang, Mama," Donovan said after enjoying a mouthful of dark meat and licking his fingers. "You know I don't like fowl."

"What was that?" Genevieve drily replied. "I couldn't hear what you said around all that smacking on that *bird* you don't like!"

Everyone at the table laughed.

"You and Granny are the only ones who can make us eat food we abhor," Diamond commented as she enjoyed a forkful of squash. "Remember how I thought I hated parsnips and I'd been eating them for years?"

"How can I forget?" Mary replied, with a laugh. "I'm the one who kept telling you they were spicy potatoes!"

"Well, I've never met a food I don't like," Dexter piped in, after following a heaping forkful of greens with a bite of corn bread. "That's why no matter how fine my woman is... she's got to be able to cook!"

Diamond raised her eyebrow. "Oh, really? Well, considering the skinny, silicone-injected Barbie dolls you prefer, who don't look like they even eat...good luck with that."

"My women aren't skinny. They're just in shape."

"That chick he was with on Friday had quite a figure," Donovan said. "What was her name, Dex?"

"Maria. Maria Sanchez."

"She's a beautiful woman."

Dexter nodded. "I agree, brother."

Genevieve eyed her son curiously. "Boy, you have a new girlfriend every week. Are we crossing the border this time around?"

"You know me, Ma. I'm an equal-opportunity lover."

"Watch yourself there, boy," Grandfather David warned. "You've got respectable women around this table." After a pause, he continued. "That's a cigar-and-brandy conversation for men alone."

Mary looked at the husband she'd loved for almost sixty years. "Oh, so you're not saying, don't talk like that? You're saying, don't talk like that around the womenfolk? Is that it?"

David's eyes twinkled. "That's it exactly."

"Ooh, no, he didn't," Genevieve said with a laugh. "He's keeping secrets from you, Ma." It was just like her father-in-law to stir things up. There was never a dull moment when a group of Drake men sat around a table.

Mary looked at Genevieve. "Child, I'm not worried. Anything he doesn't share at the table he'll spill in the bedroom."

"Watch yourself, now, Granny," Diamond said, mimicking

her grandfather. "That sounds like a kitchen conversation for women only!"

"It is, baby. And I'll give you the full 411 so you can know how to handle your man."

"Wait!" Dexter's laughter filled the room. "Did my eighty-year-old grandmother just say 411, as in *information?*"

"I'm seventy-eight," Mary responded, eyes twinkling. "Don't push me, now."

Diamond leaned over and hugged Mary. "My granny is in the know!"

"Speaking of in the know," Donovan said cryptically. "Why don't you tell us about your new man?"

Seven sets of eyes looked at Diamond.

*Oh, Lord. Here we go.* "I do not have a new man," Diamond corrected. "That's what you get for trying to be all up in my business."

"You'd better tell him that," Donovan replied. "Because on Friday night, Jackson was looking at you like a piece of prime real estate that he'd like to own!"

"Please, Donovan," Diamond replied, deadpan. "Stop with the histrionics. First of all, Jackson wasn't looking at me in any particular way, and second, nobody owns me!"

"Hmm," Papa Dee said, speaking up for the first time since picking up his fork and beginning to eat. "Me thinks the lady doth protest too much!"

Diamond got ready to argue and then thought better of it. Who could ever win an argument against someone who'd been on the planet for almost a century?

Donald wiped his mouth with a napkin, then reared back with his glass of wine. "Are we talking about Boss Wright, as in the owner of Boss Construction?"

Donovan nodded. "He was at the benefit Friday night, sniffing behind Diamond like a rottweiler."

"Just make sure his bark is worth his bite," Mary said.

Diamond frowned. *Huh?*

Genevieve explained. "While he talks the talk, make sure he can walk the walk. You could do worse than a successful, wealthy man," she continued. "You're over twenty-nine. It's time you settled down. It's time that all of you get cured of singleitis," she continued, pointedly looking at all three of her children. "Yes, even you," she said to Dexter, when he would have argued. "I had all of you by the time I turned thirty. At the rate you three are going, I'll be Papa's age before I see grandchildren."

Papa Dee chuckled. "Lord, I hope not. You wouldn't be able to bounce them on creaking knees like mine!"

"Do you think this could get serious?" Genevieve asked Diamond.

"There is nothing happening to get serious! Seeing Jackson, Boss, whatever he calls himself, at the benefit was purely coincidental. Donovan is reading way too much into the fact that he and I were conversing. Now can we please change the subject? You guys are starting to get on my nerves."

Donald obliged his daughter and shifted the focus from weddings and babies to wines and spreadsheets. But that didn't stop Donovan from cornering her just before he left the house.

"I've got a question, sis."

Diamond stifled a sigh. When it came to older brothers, sometimes there was a thin line between love and hate. "What?"

"If nothing is happening between you and Jackson, why did you not bring the beer you offered to get, text me about some jive pop-up headache, and then seconds later I watch homeboy return to his seat with a smug look on his face?"

"I don't know, brother. Why don't you ask Jackson?"

"Because I'm asking you."

"I'm a grown woman, Donovan. Which is why you really need to mind your own business."

"You heard what Mama said about wanting us to get married, and I know that's what you want, as well." Donovan stepped closer to his sister and further lowered his voice. "For the record, I don't think your boy Jackson is the marrying kind."

## Chapter 9

The next day, Diamond was more than ready to jump into work. Between what little sleep she'd gotten and her mother's interrogation after the brothers had left, it was a miracle that she'd survived the weekend at all—that and the fact that she'd actually dreamed of Jackson. Diamond blushed at the thought.

"Good morning, darlin'!"

"Morning, Kat." Diamond walked up to Kathleen's desk and reached for the typed agenda that sat on her desk. "Looks like somebody had a happy weekend."

"It was amazing. The old codger gave me an early Christmas present. We're going to Ireland!"

"Wow, Kathleen, that *is* amazing. Bernie must have gotten a raise. When are you going?"

"That's why he had to surprise me early. We need to lock in the dates and are hoping to go around the holidays."

Diamond looked up. "As long as it's not Thanksgiving, our new opening weekend, I think we'll be fine."

"You're a diamond, Diamond."

Diamond rolled her eyes. "Whatever."

"Oh, shoot. I was so excited about the Ireland trip that I almost forgot. There was a message on the phone when I arrived. It might be important."

Diamond's stomach flip-flopped. *Jackson?* "Who from?"

"*O Magazine.* The message is in your Microsoft Outlook, along with the others."

"Thanks, Kat." Diamond walked into her office. Before she could sit down, Kat buzzed her on the intercom. "Line one for you, Diamond."

"Who is it?"

"Jackson Wright."

Kathleen hurriedly disconnected the call. Diamond knew why—she would have insisted that Kathleen take a message. Kathleen hanging up was her way of saying, put on your big-girl britches and take the call.

Today, Diamond's "britches" were an ivory-colored Chanel suit, its sleek, formfitting lines subtly accenting her curves. Her ivory pumps and three-strand pearls were classic, while her spiky do lessened the conservativeness of the total look.

Diamond took a breath and put on the last piece of attire needed before answering the phone: a professional demeanor. She punched the speaker button and spoke in a cool, crisp tone. "Diamond Drake."

Jackson laughed, and Diamond was at once irritated. It was the same sound she'd heard Friday night when commenting that their relationship was strictly business. In Diamond's mind, it was the sound of confidence and cockiness, as if Jackson just knew he was the cat's meow. Then she remembered Friday night: music, full moon, smooth jazz, skilled kisses and how her cat had meowed. She clamped her legs together and continued in a huff. "What is so humorous about my name?"

"Not your name, baby," Jackson said, a smile in his voice even though his heart beat at a million miles per hour. "Your attitude. I know you're a consummate professional, baby. You don't have to prove anything to me."

"If you know that, then one, why are you calling me during office hours, and two, why are you calling me *baby* when you should address me as either Diamond or Ms. Drake?"

"Very well," Jackson conceded, his voice taking on a businesslike tone. "Ms. Drake."

Diamond closed her eyes and fought the wave of desire that swept over her. *How is it that he can say my name so professionally yet squeeze sexuality between each consonant and vowel?* With each interaction of the Jackson Wright kind, Diamond was becoming more disconcerted. She'd never before reacted this strongly to a man, never felt such a magnetic pull to another human being. And with all that was presently on her plate, now was not the time! "Yes, Mr. Wright," she said when control once again returned. She stopped short of asking, What can I do for you? But she believed she already knew his answer to that question.

"I just got off the phone with Taylor Stevens. She's requested a meeting tomorrow night, to go over the proposed changes to the restaurant's design that we discussed after the walk-through. I think it would be a good idea for you to join us."

"Thanks, Jackson, but I've already approved those changes. There's no reason for me to be there."

"It may be a time-saver in the long run," Jackson responded. "The change to the roof is extensive. Since I know you're running this project, yours will be valuable input to our meeting."

"Yes, I'm in charge of it now, but Donovan handled the

first phase and Dexter has been kept in the loop, as well. Perhaps one of them is available."

There was a brief pause before Jackson responded. "I understand." He gave Diamond the meeting location information and ended the call.

Diamond immediately dialed Donovan. "Hey, Don."

"Diamond, what's up?"

"Remember the addition Taylor suggested, the one about incorporating a glass ceiling to the lounge area that extends into the garden?"

"Right."

Diamond could hear Donovan shuffling papers in the background, as well as the hurriedness in his voice. She got right to the point. "Taylor and Jackson are having a meeting tomorrow night. They want one of us to be there."

"No can do, sis. I have a meeting with the distributors for the restaurants." As the innovative VP of sales, Donovan had recently secured a lucrative contract with a midlevel restaurant chain. The Drake line would be unveiled there during the holidays.

Diamond hid her disappointment. "No worries. I'll ask Dex."

"He's not here."

"Where is he?"

"In Vegas, mixing business with pleasure. He'll be back the day after tomorrow. Look, sis, I have another call. I've got to go."

Diamond let out a sigh as she hung up the phone. She knew she was being irrational, but there was no way she was ready to face Jackson again. It was too soon after their encounter. She could still feel his hands caressing her buttocks, could still taste his lips. *I'll talk to Taylor. She can handle this.* With the decision made, Diamond reached for the folder containing the advertising company's promo of the second leg of the Drake holiday campaign beginning next month. She'd seen the ads and reviewed the commercial several times but wanted to incorporate the theme into the company's November newsletter. Happy to take her mind off Jackson by letting her creative juices flow, Diamond dove into writing and was just hitting her groove when her intercom buzzed.

"Yes, Kat."

"Line one, Diamond. It's *O Magazine*."

"Okay, I'll take it. Thanks." Diamond punched the flashing white light. "Diamond Drake." Thirty minutes later, she sat stunned yet excited. *O Magazine* wanted to do a four-page spread on Drake Wines Resort & Spa and not only that but the queen of daytime talk was planning a visit, the filming of which could end up as a special on OWN. She squealed, and after sharing the news with Kat, she walked to her father's office.

"Dad! You'll never guess what just happened."

Donald looked up from the report he was reading, looking very much the part of a successful company COO. "No, but I have a feeling you're going to tell me."

"We're going to be featured in *O Magazine!*" She relayed what the magazine editor had shared with her, including the fact that Oprah Winfrey wanted to visit their vineyard during the holiday season.

"That's great news, honey," Donald said. "When is this supposed to take place?"

"That's the one tiny hitch in the giddyup," Diamond said. "They want to feature us in one of their summer issues, which means the shoot and interviews can happen no later than January or February."

"Well, having been opened a couple months at that point we should have everything in place."

"I think so, but I'm even more determined to finish the construction on schedule so that we can focus on interior design." Diamond's eyes narrowed with a realization. In order to make sure the renovation was finished and the interior design flawless, she'd have to stay more involved in the renovation than she'd planned. There was no way she'd be able to avoid Jackson—at least for the next four weeks. "I've got a meeting tomorrow night with Jackson and Taylor. Now, along with the last-minute changes we've proposed, I need to let them know that we'll need to implement those changes and complete this project by the third week in November. No excuses, no exceptions."

"That's only four weeks away. Can we do it?"

"We'll have to—even if it means increasing the budget to double the crews."

"Well, baby girl, if anybody can make it happen, it's you."

"Thanks, Dad."

"One more thing, Diamond."

"Yes, Dad."

"Since you're working late tomorrow night, try and take some time off later this week. You're becoming a workaholic, like your old man."

"All right, Dad. I'll think about it." As Diamond left her father's office, she felt confident that everyone would rise to the challenge and make this new deadline. She only wished she were as certain that she could behave herself at the meeting tomorrow night…and keep her hands off Jackson.

# Chapter 10

The next evening, Diamond arrived at the restaurant on schedule and quickly found a parking space near the building. She wore her power business suit, and, while she'd convinced herself that this had nothing to do with whom she was meeting, she'd freshened her makeup and sleeked down the short do she was still getting used to.

The waiter led her to the table that Jackson occupied. He stood as she approached. "Ms. Drake."

"All right, Jackson." She sat. "You may call me Diamond."

"As you wish." Jackson sat, as well. "But you very much look like Ms. Drake right now, up to that sleek hairstyle and down to your sexy heels. I really like your hair short like that. It looks good."

The waiter interrupted. "Would you like to place a drink order?"

"We're waiting for another person," Diamond quickly replied, thinking that the last thing she needed was alcohol

This man's looks alone made her feel tipsy. *I've got to keep my wits about me.*

"While we wait, I think I'll have a glass of cabernet," Jackson said. Mr. Bravado concealed the nervousness he hadn't felt since he'd asked Misty Adams to meet him behind the skating rink: a request that had ended in his loss of virginity. There was something about Diamond Drake that brought out his chivalry and need to protect, along with every insecurity he'd ever known. "Would you like one, Diamond?"

"I'll take a glass of sparkling water with lemon slices." She quickly shifted the focus to business. "Did Taylor forward the ideas we discussed last week?"

Jackson nodded. "I had my architect draw up some diagrams to present. As soon as... Ah, here she is." Jackson stood as Taylor approached the table. Both he and Diamond immediately noticed her demeanor. "Are you okay?"

"No," Taylor said, sitting quickly. "I don't know what it is about this project and disturbing phone calls, but I got another just now as I was parking my car. My dad was en route to meet some friends for dinner. There was an accident."

Jackson's brow creased.

"Taylor," Diamond said, placing a hand on Taylor's arm. "Is he all right?"

"We don't know," Taylor replied, shaking her head. "Yes, I'd like a glass of your top-shelf merlot, please," she said to the waiter who approached their table. And then back to Diamond, she said, "My sister called on her way to the hospital. We're trying to stay optimistic at this point."

"Taylor, we'll totally understand you having to leave this meeting." Jackson's voice was filled with concern. "You must be worried sick."

"Our family's pretty dramatic," Taylor said with a nervous laugh. "It could be a fender bender and an APB would still be sent out to all corners of the globe." The waiter arrived, and Taylor took a healthy gulp from her wineglass. The trio passed on appetizers for the moment and instead tried to focus on work. But it wasn't meant to be. A couple minutes later, Taylor's phone rang. She nodded as she listened to the person on the other end of the phone. "That's good news, but I still want to see him," she said. After hanging up the phone, she began gathering the items she'd placed on the table. "That was my sister. Dad is going to be fine. There were no internal or life-threatening injuries. But there's still no way I can concentrate tonight," she said to Diamond with an apologetic smile. "So sorry to have to run out on you guys, but I'm the consummate daddy's girl."

"I totally understand," Diamond said, knowing that if she'd heard that her father was in an accident, she'd feel the same way. "I'm glad to know that it wasn't more serious."

When Taylor stood, Jackson did, as well. "Sorry to hear about your father, but I, too, am very glad he's okay."

"Thanks, Jackson."

"And when you see your father, give him a hug."

Taylor smiled at Jackson. "I sure will."

Jackson and Diamond watched Taylor rush out of the restaurant. When he sat, Jackson's mood was somber. They ordered appetizers and tried to continue the meeting, but his mind was obviously elsewhere. "Maybe we should continue this discussion another time," Diamond finally said.

"Sorry," Jackson replied. "The news that Taylor received—and the way she received it—hit close to home."

Diamond was used to seeing cockiness and swagger when she looked at Jackson. But now she saw something else—vulnerability. "Do you want to talk about it?"

For a while, it seemed as though Jackson's answer was no. When he began speaking, his voice was low, his eyes downcast. "I lost the people who raised me almost seven years ago," he said, idly fingering the water glass before him. "It was a car wreck."

Jackson looked at Diamond. Her heart clenched at the pain she saw in his eyes. "Oh, Jackson, that must have been terrible."

Jackson nodded, remembering experiences that had been equally as devastating: his mother's drug use, for instance, and his brushes with the law. "A drag-racing teenager killed my aunt Evie and uncle John, who'd built the construction company I own from the ground up. He taught me almost everything I know, especially how to be a man. Had it not been for my uncle's influence, my life would probably look very different from what it does now."

"And someone called you about their accident?"

"I was in a club partying, getting my groove on when I got the call that changed my life." Jackson sat back in the booth, looked beyond Diamond into the worst day of his life. "I'd intended to visit them that day but went on an impromptu date instead." The smile on Jackson's face was fleeting and bittersweet. "I never got a chance for that last hug, you know? Never got to say goodbye."

For the first time since meeting him, Diamond initiated contact. She reached over and placed a comforting hand on Jackson's arm. "I'm sorry."

Jackson shrugged, putting his Teflon veneer firmly back in place. "Death is a part of life."

Diamond was silent, finding it impossible to imagine a life without Donald and Genevieve Drake. The kids often joked with their parents that they had to at least outlive Papa Dee, who was two years shy of one hundred. "Do you have siblings?"

"No."

The dark look crossed Jackson's face so quickly that Diamond thought she'd imagined it. It occurred to her how little she knew about Jackson Wright. But now felt like an inappropriate time for questions. She looked at her watch. "I should be going. Is there any way we can continue this meeting Thursday, at the site?"

"Can I confirm that morning? I don't know what's going on until Marissa tells me."

"Marissa?"

"My assistant."

"Oh, okay."

Jackson smiled for the first time in several minutes. "You thought I was talking about my woman or wife?"

"No, I—"

"Ha! Yes, you did."

There it was…that irritating chuckle. Here was the Jackson that Diamond had come to know, the one who helped her remember that she didn't like him, wasn't attracted to him and wasn't interested in anything more than business when it came to him. "Look, I don't care who Melissa—"

"*Marissa,* Marissa Hayes. She's been my assistant since I took over the business six years ago."

*Is that a smile or a smirk on his face?* Diamond took a surreptitious breath to calm her ire. No man had ever gotten her this hot, in anger or desire. *I'm not going to give him the satisfaction of thinking he's upset me. I'm not jealous! I couldn't care less about Marissa!* "Thanks for the company history," Diamond nonchalantly replied in a tone that her mother, the queen of dry, would be proud of. "If you're free, around one o'clock Thursday will work for me. If I'm not available, you can leave a message with my assistant, Kathleen Fitzpatrick. She's been with the company for twenty years."

With that, Diamond walked out of the restaurant with her head held high. But it was not fast enough to escape the sound of Jackson's low, soft chuckle that tickled her back the way his fingers had three days before.

# Chapter 11

"My, don't we look lovely," Kathleen said as soon as Diamond entered the office.

"I look the same as always, Kat."

"It's understandable," Kathleen continued, her fingers flying across the keyboard and eyes glued to the screen, "since that handsome construction fellow is meeting you for lunch."

This news stopped Diamond in her tracks. "Jackson called?" Of course, she'd hoped he would. That's why she'd taken special care with her wardrobe and added an extra spray of perfume to the day's preparations, her "same as always" comment notwithstanding. She'd hoped that these extra touches would come off casual and nonchalant. She wore a tan-colored pencil skirt with a billowy floral top that cinched at the waist. The neckline was tasteful yet hinted at treasures. She returned her short hair to its spiky form. It was just another day at the office—no big deal. But Kathleen had noticed. "We mentioned meeting today at one o'clock," Diamond continued, "but we didn't discuss lunch."

"I assumed it would be a lunch meeting since that's how you generally handle clients who meet between noon and two."

"Did you mention that to him?"

"No."

"Good. We'll meet at the site and then, if necessary, come back to the office."

"So I shouldn't set up a spread in the conference room?"

"No, Kat, but thank you for asking." *Jeez, what is with this woman? Doesn't she know that just seeing Jackson stirs up an entirely different kind of appetite?*

Diamond went into her office. Four hours passed in which Diamond had no idea what she did. Floating on autopilot was an understatement. All she could think about was the dichotomy that was Jackson Wright: the superassured macho man she'd first met juxtaposed with the caring, vulnerable human being she'd glimpsed Tuesday night, after hearing the news about Taylor's dad. Wafting through these thoughts were the memories that had rarely left her since the concert: his kiss. By the time Kathleen buzzed to let her know that Jackson had arrived, Diamond was a composed, organized, calm-looking mess.

When Jackson entered her office, Diamond came around her desk. "Hello, Jackson."

"Ms. Drake," Jackson replied, looking absolutely decadent in black jeans, red shirt and cowboy boots.

*Cowboy boots? When it comes to Mr. Wright, will the surprises ever end?*

In the most utmost act of professionalism, he reached out for a handshake. "It's good to see you again."

"You just saw me Tuesday night," Diamond answered, hoping that she sounded appropriately relaxed. "Let's set up here, at the conference table. Once I'm sure we're on the same page, we can go to the site." She missed Kathleen's confused expression, having totally forgotten that mere moments ago she'd informed Kathleen that the exact opposite would occur.

Jackson followed Diamond to the area of her large L-shaped office that housed an oval conference table. While he'd vowed that unlike during other encounters he would be the "strictly business" brother Diamond said she wanted, he couldn't help but notice how the skirt she wore cupped her luscious booty the way his hands longed to, couldn't stop remembering how his hands felt buried in her hair. He thought of other things he'd like to bury in other places before forcing away the train of thought and the inevitable evidence of desire that would embarrass them both.

"Nice office," he said, eating up the distance to the table with long, sure strides and placing his briefcase on the table. "Did Taylor design it?"

"No. We didn't meet her until this renovation. Her credentials are impeccable and awards impressive. But then again, seeing as you're in the building profession, I might be telling you something that you already know."

"Taylor Stevens isn't famous yet, but in the architectural community, she's a household name." Jackson spread the drawings on the table as he talked. "We've worked together in the past, and I can tell you that these are some of the most ambitious plans I've seen from her."

"Even so, we need to kick things up another notch."

Jackson raised his brow in question.

Diamond told him about the call from *O Magazine.* "I'm totally in love with what we've planned so far. If you have any further ideas that would add to this site's uniqueness, I'm open."

Jackson's eyes darkened at thoughts of the woman before him being open and in love. "Come here," he commanded,

changing the subject along with his demeanor—still professional, but with just enough sexy thrown into his voice to
make Diamond's heart skip a beat. "I want to show you how
I'm going to make all of your dreams come true."

Diamond's breath caught in her throat. What she was
dreaming about in this moment had absolutely nothing to do
with Drake Wines Resort & Spa and everything to do with
the man standing next to her. He evoked in her images best
left forgotten, like diamond rings and wedding bells, silk
dresses with shoes dyed to match. In her mind's eye, Diamond saw Jackson sauntering down the aisle, his bow askew,
that lovable, cocky smile on his face. She almost moaned
aloud. *Strictly professional. That's how I roll. No colleagues
or playboys.* Ignoring the sudden wetness between her legs,
she walked closer to where Jackson was standing.

"I propose that we install a glass ceiling, from the fireplace
and front sitting area—" Jackson's long, tapered finger slid
across the paper "—all the way to here, the second sitting
area where the piano bar and Stage B will be erected."

Jackson continued with his explanation, but Diamond
didn't hear it. All she could do was feel the heat emanating
from his body and imagine how it would feel on top of her.
His hand rested on the paper, and she imagined it massaging her body, imagined sucking his fingers into her mouth,
one by one and imagined setting him as on fire as she was
right now. Even with her three-inch heels, Jackson was still
taller, with a virility that oozed out of his pores. There had
been other moments of celibacy in her life, and never before
had she been so flustered; never before had she wanted a man
as much as she wanted this one. Now all she had to do was
make sure that Jackson never found this out.

"Diamond? Are you listening?"

"Of course. I agree that an expanded glass ceiling is a
wonderful idea. What's the added cost?" Jackson looked at

her and smiled. A smile like that should come with a warning label and sirens or something to give a sister a chance to brace herself. "Did I say something funny?"

"Your question would have made sense two sentences ago—when I threw out a proposed figure for the upgrade, along with the fact that I'd already brought additional proposals for your dad and the finance department."

There was no comment for that one; Diamond buried her embarrassment under the pretense of studying the drawings on the table. And what was it about being near this man that made her lose her hearing?

"The accelerated schedule shouldn't be a problem, especially since you're willing to approve additional manpower. And with the holidays approaching, the guys will relish the work."

Diamond's office phone rang. "Hey, Dad," she said. "We were just talking about you."

"Who's we?"

"Jackson is here going over the additions we discussed. He's worked up some figures, and if you have a moment, we'd like to stop by your office."

"Ginny and I have a date tonight. So you'd best stop by now."

Diamond smiled at her father's words. Her parents had been dating for thirty-five years.

Moments later, Jackson and Diamond stepped into the massive corner office of Donald Drake. Masculinity oozed from every pore of this tycoon's body and every fiber of his office, from the dark mahogany and black leather furniture to the framed 1930 Winchester Model 12 shotgun that had been given to Papa Dee when he was sixteen. Jackson felt right at home. "Mr. Drake," he said, walking in with hand outstretched, "good to see you again."

The men exchanged a firm handshake.

"Likewise, Boss," Donald said, with a scrutinizing gaze. "And how many times have I said you can call me Donald?"

Jackson smiled. "More than once, sir."

"All right, then. I toured the site again yesterday, and I must tell you that I've never seen finer workmanship."

"Thank you, sir."

"I wasn't too crazy about your idea of the stone-rock setting for the Jacuzzis, but it works. Makes it look as though those pools spring right from the ground."

"I'm glad you're satisfied."

"More than pleased, son."

*Son.* And again, visions of wedding bells danced in her head. Diamond gave it a subtle shake. She was more than a little troubled at the effect Jackson had on her. She wasn't thinking about relationships right now, let alone marriage. And when she did, it would be to someone logical and practical, not to this stallion standing tall beside her, the one who made her lose her mind. And losing it she was. Why else would she be standing here with thoughts that were delusional?

"Dad, we have the drawings for the glass ceiling I discussed with you." Diamond walked toward Donald's large desk as she spoke. They viewed the drawings, discussed the upgrades and then, as Jackson and Diamond prepared to leave his office, Donald made a suggestion that suggested to Diamond that she wasn't the only crazy in the room.

"Jackson, I know you've tasted our wine, but have you perused our vineyard?"

"No, Donald, I haven't."

Donald looked at his daughter. "Diamond, why don't you give Jackson the grand tour?"

# Chapter 12

Jackson and Diamond left Donald's office and, after stopping by Diamond's office for the key to the golf cart used to tour the grounds, headed for the parking lot. "I thought Dexter had shown you the grounds," Diamond said, trying to still her rapidly beating heart. The thought of her and Jackson alone between large, shielding grapevines away from the hubbub of the business had all kinds of thoughts ping-ponging inside her head. "This is such an inspiring piece of property that it's sure to further enhance the skills you and your team are bringing to the renovation."

"Oh, so you're interested in my skills, huh?" Jackson teased.

"Are you always so cocky?" Diamond cut Jackson a look. "Behave."

They reached the golf cart as Jackson replied, "I make no such promises, sweetheart. Beautiful day spent in a beautiful vineyard with a beautiful woman?" He turned sultry eyes on Diamond's lips as he licked his own. "Anything can happen."

Diamond started the cart. "Anything" couldn't happen fast enough. In this moment, it was decided. She was going to sleep with this man. It was either that or lose her mind, and there was no way she could do that with a building project that needed to be completed in thirty days and Oprah's people arriving two months after that. She knew just where the seduction would take place. *Now. Today. Rules be damned!* Of course, these thoughts were fleeting. There was positively no way she could be with this man. No way!

"Ideally I'd start the tour at the eastern edge of the vineyard," she said as she came to a stop in front of a large farm-like structure just down the lane from the executive offices. "But since we're so close, let's start here, our shipping headquarters. The wines are stored in the cellar below it." She hopped out of the cart, and without waiting to see if Jackson followed her, she walked to the ornately decorated double doors.

She and Jackson stepped inside and it was if they'd entered a large showroom housing row after row and case after case of wines that were ready for shipment. "Wow," Jackson said, whistling softly. "This is impressive."

Diamond smiled, her chest swelling with pride. "This is the heartbeat of Drake Wines, where the wines are housed once they're bottled." They began walking down a long, wide aisle. "The wines are shelved by type and year, beginning with the whites, reds, burgundies and then moving on to the sparkling varieties."

They reached the last aisle, and Jackson noticed a stairway. "Where do those steps lead?"

Diamond looked at Jackson. "The cellar," she said, a bit breathlessly. "That's where the wines are aged. Now, on to the vineyards."

"Aged in those large oak barrels, like we see in the movies?"

"Yes," Diamond said, over her shoulder, taking into account the fact that Jackson hadn't moved. "They are sixty-gallon containers made from premium oak."

"I want to see them."

"We don't have much time." She was halfway to the door.

"Unless you're scared."

*Screech.*

This is how she'd ended up climbing trees, eating bugs and lying facedown in a shallow creek bed, covered with mud—because her brothers had dared her. She should have learned her lesson. But "should" was on vacation and "would" turned around and marched back to where Jackson stood.

Determined to wipe the smirk off of his face, she squared her shoulders and sounded as businesslike as she could with wet panties. "Follow me."

She started down the stairs. Jackson's eyes darkened as he watched her from behind. Actually, as he watched her behind…the way the pencil skirt caressed each cheek that clenched—first left, then right—with each step she took. He felt himself harden and did nothing to control his ardor. He wanted Diamond, pure and simple. And he wanted her now.

They reached the bottom step, where there was a small landing with heavy metal doors on three sides. "Different rooms are used to house the different wines," she explained matter-of-factly. "The temperatures vary depending on which grape is being used but for the most part hover around fifty-eight degrees." Even as she said this, she realized that her thermometer had been stuck on one setting since first laying eyes on Jackson Wright…hot. *I will not give this man the satisfaction of seducing me,* she vowed, after unlocking and then opening one of the doors. *That's probably what he's used to, what he expects.* Determined to control her uncontrollable passion for him, she took a calming breath and turned around. "These barrels—"

Jackson swallowed Diamond's gasp as the lips he'd claimed the moment she turned parted and welcomed his tongue. The kiss was forceful, demanding—his hands searching, finding, massaging soft flesh. He wrapped strong arms around her before burying one hand in her soft, spiky hair and using his other one to press her against his burgeoning manhood. His tongue mimicked the hips that were grinding against her, leaving no doubt as to what he desired. He ran his hand up her back and around to the soft breasts crushed against his chest. Brushing a finger against the soft material that hid part of her treasure, he smiled when a hardened nipple was his instant reward. But there was a problem: too much fabric between them. Thrusting his tongue deeper, Jackson reached for the belt that cinched Diamond's blouse at her waist. One would have thought he'd designed it—so quickly was he able to undo the clasp. *Butter*. That's what Diamond's skin felt like. It was silky smooth and on fire. He placed his hand on her lacy bra, rubbed her areola through the fabric and then he tweaked it.

Diamond came undone.

She reached for the hem of her blouse and broke the kiss just long enough to pull the silky fabric over her head. She noticed that Jackson's chocolate-brown orbs were black with desire. What she didn't know was that they mirrored her own. Resuming the kiss, she wrapped her arms around Jackson's neck, crushing her breasts against his chest. But there was just one problem. There were still too many clothes. She reached for Jackson's T-shirt, pulling it out of his jeans. Taking the hint, Jackson quickly shed it, tossing it in the direction Diamond's blouse had gone.

"I want to make love to you," he murmured, sending a trail of kisses from her mouth to her neck and back. "Now."

It was time to wave the white flag, throw in the towel and join the one she couldn't beat. "Me, too." She reached behind her and unzipped her skirt. Shimmying out of it and enjoying the freedom, she reached behind her and unsnapped her bra. Her breasts seemed to cheer, swaying their silent invitation.

Jackson was quick to RSVP. He rubbed one nipple and licked the other, lapping as if it oozed Drake Wines' pinot noir 2002, one of the vineyard's most popular winners. His fingers found the edge of her thong, and one of them slid inside, running along the folds of her pleasure then slipping inside for a more thorough greeting. Diamond's head dropped back, her legs spread of their own volition. Another finger slipped inside, and he began playing her box like she was a piano and he was Duke Ellington. Taking the "A" train would have been too fast. So Jackson tapped her like a satin doll, and her slippery folds mimicked that material. She moaned, grinding herself against Jackson's hand. He felt her hand slide up his leg and rest on his massive package. She squeezed him through the thick jean fabric.

And Jackson came undone.

Picking up Diamond as if she were a feather, he walked them to a row of barrels, placed Diamond on top of one and dropped to his knees. He spread her legs and placed soft kisses on alternating thighs. He felt Diamond's hands rubbing the soft black curls on his head. It spurred him on and up her leg, where, after spreading her wider, he licked her through the lacy thong that matched the bra that was now who knew where. She hissed. Jackson chuckled that cocky, knowing laugh. *Yeah, I'm on to something, baby girl. And I'm just getting started.* With the precision of a fencer's sword, his tongue tickled her nub. After a love bite on the same sweetness, he moved aside the lace and got down to business, reaching, it seemed, for Diamond's core.

And found it.

Diamond's legs began to quiver as an orgasm uncoiled from the pit of her paradise and spread throughout her entire body. She'd never experienced such an intense sensation, never witnessed such mastery of the oral organ in her life. She heard mewling, whimpers, and then realized that these sounds were coming from her own mouth. Feeling as limp as an abandoned double-Dutch rope, she slumped against Jackson's shoulder.

Jackson uttered three words, "I'm not finished." And Diamond's vajayjay began tingling all over again.

## *Chapter 13*

He stood and kissed her leisurely, thoroughly, the taste of Diamond's essence on his tongue. He stepped back, and she felt bereft and abandoned, her thoughts scattered like ashes in the wind. Then Jackson's jeans and boxers fell to the cement floor and brought Diamond's attention into laser focus. Was that for real, and if so...was that all for her?

Jackson's hardened, engorged shaft stood proudly before him, swaying from its own weightiness. Diamond's mouth watered, and her swallow was audible.

A small smile scampered across his face as, like a panther on the prowl, he walked back to her. "Do you want this?"

Diamond's eyes never left his as she nodded. She couldn't get any words past the constriction in her chest. And really, what was there to say? She'd thank Santa later for Christmas in October. This man was a gift, and right now she didn't even care if he knew that she knew it. She let the longing show openly on her face as she watched him open the condom foil and wrap his package. Diamond swallowed again and licked her lips. In one fell swoop, Jackson picked her off the barrel, which was a good thing since her legs still resembled the abandoned double-Dutch rope. She wrapped her legs just above his perfectly round derriere, noting its hardness and making a mental note to take a closer examination at a later date. He walked them to the wall, penned her against it, and then the dance began in earnest.

He stroked her slowly, inch by excruciatingly beautiful inch, allowing her body time to adjust to his sizable girth. Diamond's fingernails dug into his shoulders as she absorbed a myriad of sensations, including the realization that nothing in her romantic life had prepared her for this moment.

It took a while before he was fully inside her, but at the moment he settled flush against her, Jackson thought that he'd died and gone to heaven. And if that were so, this brother never wanted his feet to touch earth again. He sighed with contentment, turning his head to capture Diamond's mouth in a scorching kiss. His tongue made leisurely circles inside her hot mouth, and soon his hips were moving in a circular motion.

Not to be outdone, Diamond's hips duplicated his motion, and her core ignited. Jackson pulled out, teased her with the tip of his penis and then plunged back in again—seemingly even deeper than before. Was it possible for a man to grow two additional inches on the spot? If not, this was the day for miracles, because Diamond swore that was what happened. He tickled her core with his determination; over and again he touched her there…slow and purposeful, fast and sure. His body tingled all over as he felt her kissing every part of his face. Emotions he swore were beneath him came rushing to the surface—emotions that spoke of commitment and loyalty and forever.

Once again, Diamond's legs began to shake from the

strength of his desire and her conviction. It was as if her very breath was being taken away but she still managed to cry out as he pumped harder. Faster. Deeper. *Damn!* Her climax was meteorological, complete with stars and flashes of lightning. She had never been a screamer, but now short bursts of sound bounced off the cement walls as wave after wave after wave of ecstasy washed over her. Tears came to her eyes at the beauty of it all. After a series of staccato thrusts, Jackson joined her in the afternoon cataclysmic paradise they'd created. Had there been an audience, they would have stomped their feet in standing ovation and demanded an encore. Jackson wanted an encore his damn self!

"What's that sound?" Diamond asked, once she'd summoned enough strength to open her mouth.

"My phone," Jackson replied. He'd heard the vibration several times during the course of their lovemaking but had tuned out all but the feel of being inside Diamond's delectable body. Yet now he admitted that since it was the middle of a business day and he was the owner of a multimillion-dollar company, he just might want to answer. It could be important.

He eased out of Diamond and set her on the ground as if she were a delicate, priceless piece of blown glass. He kissed her lightly on the mouth and then walked away.

Diamond watched Jackson stride across the room in all of his naked glory and retrieve the phone from the holder on his jeans. Indeed, his ass was all that and a case of Drake's finest grape, but she quelled the urge to join him where he stood and give it the massaging it seemed to be calling for. He was trying to handle business, after all. So instead, she walked on still-shaky legs in search of the thong that had been carelessly tossed aside. Her stomach rumbled, and she realized that the calories from her light lunch had been more than expended. She thought that if Jackson's schedule allowed it, she'd suggest they share an early dinner and then, maybe, go somewhere clandestine and have each other for dessert. She found her thong, and while daydreaming of Jackson and Diamond, Part II, she donned it and her bra, skirt and blouse. So deep was she in this daydream that she didn't notice that Jackson had dressed quickly as well and that the face that just moments before shone with the afterglow of serious lovemaking was now etched with unease.

"Is everything all right?"

"No," Jackson said, already heading toward the stairs. "Everything is not all right. I've got to go."

"Jackson!" Diamond called to his rapidly retreating back. But without a backward glance he was up the steps and through the door. Diamond marched up the stairs in her bare feet ready to demand an answer and, considering what they'd both just experienced, a more proper goodbye. No matter what the person on the phone had just told him, how could he just up and leave like she was already yesterday's news? "Jackson!" she called out again as she entered the large warehouse. She hurried down the aisle toward the double doors, but as she neared the front of the building, her eyes told her what her heart already knew…he was gone.

# Chapter 14

Jackson reached the Boss Construction parking lot and swerved into his reserved space. The thirty minutes that it had taken him to reach the office—when under the legal speed limit it would have taken at least forty-five—had done nothing to cool his ire. He'd mentally kicked himself for not answering the phone earlier and potentially putting both his valued assistant and his business in even more danger. It wasn't like he was an eighteen-year-old teenager with raging hormones. Why hadn't he answered his phone when he'd heard it vibrating through his jeans on the cement floor? He knew the reason. Because his head had been between Diamond's delicious legs, and his singular focus after that had been to place his dick there.

The elevator couldn't come soon enough, and once it reached the Boss offices on the thirty-story building's top floor, Jackson's long strides quickly ate up the distance between the lobby and the spacious corner offices with spectacular views of the Pacific Ocean on one side and downtown San Diego on the other. Once Jackson entered, however, he didn't see the illustrious tableau that painters would envy. The first thing he saw was a still-shaken Marissa sitting on the couch and his attorney, Abe Swartz, occupying one of the wingbacked chairs opposite her. Both stood when Jackson entered, and Marissa raced to his side.

"Where were you?" she asked, while in an uncharacteristic show of emotion she flung her arms around Jackson's waist. "I was so afraid." In this moment, Jackson knew that whatever had happened in his office was more serious than a threatening letter. "I hope you don't mind that I called Mr. Swartz," Marissa continued, nervously twisting the ring on her right hand. "But I didn't want to involve the police before speaking with you. I didn't know what else to do."

Jackson took a step and placed a hand on Marissa's shoulder. "I'm sorry I didn't get your calls from the beginning. I was…in a meeting, and my phone was on vibrate. You did the right thing in waiting until I got here." Jackson reached over and shook Abe's hand. "Guys, come into my office." Once there and seated, he looked back at Marissa. "Now, tell me again exactly what happened."

Marissa took a deep breath as she prepared to repeat what she'd shared via telephone as Jackson raced down the I-15. "I went to lunch around twelve-thirty, and when I got back, I noticed that Gia wasn't at the receptionist desk. This was strange only because we'd talked before I left and she'd said that she was working through lunch so that she could take off at four for her daughter's dentist appointment. I didn't think too much about it until I came back here, inserted my key and found the door already unlocked."

Jackson sat forward. "You're sure the door was unlocked."

"Positive."

"Was it open?"

"No, the door was closed, but it was definitely unlocked. That dead bolt has a distinctive click, plus if I don't put my key in just the right way, it sometimes sticks. I'd barely put my key in when I turned the knob and the door opened."

Jackson looked around the office. Everything seemed to be in its rightful place. "Were any of the file cabinets opened?"

Marissa shook her head.

"Anything missing that you can see?"

"No."

Jackson took a breath and eyed Marissa with a serious expression. "Are you sure you locked the door?"

Marissa shot out of her chair and began to pace the room. "Of course I'm sure, Boss! How many times have you told me to be sure to lock up? You've reiterated how costly it could be if some of the information on upcoming projects got into the wrong hands. I locked the door and then double-checked it, as always. It. Was. Locked!"

"All right, Marissa. I know this is alarming, but you've got to calm down. We have a situation, but since it looks like nothing was taken, I don't get why you're so upset."

"It's because of the information she didn't share with you," Abe interrupted. "I told her to wait until you got here so you could see for yourself."

The hairs on the back of Jackson's neck stood up. "See what?"

"This," Marissa said, motioning him out of his office and over to her cubicle, which was just outside his door.

Jackson rounded the corner of the wood-and-glass enclosure that afforded Marissa a modicum of privacy and saw the shattered glass that was once her computer screen, along with the bullet holes that riddled the area around it.

While still trying to take in the shock of someone firing a weapon in his office, Abe walked up and silently handed him a slip of paper. "This was placed on Marissa's chair."

Jackson glanced at Abe and took the piece of paper. His heart caught as he read the words that had been written with one of his assistant's markers: *The next bullet has your name on it. And as you can see, there will be no stopping me when I'm ready to 187 your no good snitch ass.*

*Snitch?* This definitely sounded like a word from his former life. But who from those years so long ago would want to threaten him now? And why? Jackson looked up in time to see Marissa's eyes flutter close. He didn't have to ask whether or not she'd read the note. "I'm sorry you had to find all of this," he said to her softly, his voice filled with compassion. "But I'm glad you weren't here when…whoever did this came by." He now totally understood her earlier outburst and felt like a heel for having been enjoying a little bit of heaven while his assistant was going through hell. Very few knew just how much turmoil his assistant had endured, why he'd hired her as his assistant with virtually no secretarial experience and why, after a painful incident she went through a few months ago, he was even more protective. Even fewer people in the present circles he traveled knew about Jackson's past. At first he'd hidden it to fit in with the private-school kids, and now he hid it because he felt it was no one's business. It was a part of his life that he wasn't proud of but also the part that caused the insecurity: having to fend for himself from the age of seven, not having a father or mother to guide these early, formative years and falling into a crowd whose machismo was often judged by how many pounds of crack you'd sold, places you'd robbed or people you'd killed. He'd left his old life more than a decade ago but at times still felt like he didn't belong to the life he'd fully embraced once he turned sixteen. "I'm sorry," he said again, knowing these words were not enough. But for now, they would have to do. "Let's go back into my office."

The three of them returned to Jackson's office, where he shut the door. "No one heard gunshots?" he asked Marissa.

She shook her head.

"I'm sure a silencer was used," Abe said.

Jackson nodded, his mind whirling with thoughts of who was behind the increasingly ominous threats.

"I know you want to keep this quiet," Abe said. "But a crime has been committed. It's time for the police to get involved. The place needs to be dusted for fingerprints, and the employees need to be questioned."

"No!"

Abe's eyes narrowed. His voice remained calm. "Someone came into this building, broke into your office and damaged your property…with a gun! I'd say these threats are now too close for comfort, Jackson."

"If news leaks out about any of this, especially the part that involves weapons, the press will have a field day. They'll turn finding a bullet hole into some kind of gang activity. You know how small this industry is, how easily a bid can be swayed from one company to the next. I don't want to have that kind of negative publicity." What he said was true, but that wasn't all of it. Though it was irrational, a part of Jackson was ashamed of his old life: the things he'd done and the plight of his mother. There was a slight yet undeniable fear that if all of the truth ever came out, his empire could disappear just as rapidly as it had come to him. He and Marissa shared a look, one that Abe Swartz observed. "We have to keep a lid on this."

Abe leaned more comfortably into the large leather chair that sat opposite Jackson's desk. He steepled his fingers and gazed at Jackson intently. "I knew your uncle a long time," he said at last. "And I'll honor his memory by keeping this quiet, for now, and helping you as much as I can. But I'm

going to need two things from you. One, I need to know what
it is you're hiding and, two, who you've pissed off enough to
want to see you dead."

# Chapter 15

Back at Drake Wines, Diamond stewed. Her fingers itched to dial Jackson's number. But she would not. She'd rather dive headfirst into a vat of smushed grapes—fully clothed... in designer originals. She'd chided herself a thousand times for giving in to her desires, let alone the fact that she had enjoyed herself immensely while doing so. Her nether muscles clenched at the memory, and as much as she hated it, her body wanted more of Jackson "Boss" Wright. Even now she could hear him laugh, that irritatingly smug sound that hours earlier she'd deemed one of the sexiest noises she'd ever heard. Of course, at the time a certain body part was being tickled by his tongue. *Enough!* Diamond snatched up the revisions of the latest newsletter she'd printed out and forced herself to concentrate. *Yeah, right. Good luck with that.*

A light tap sounded on Diamond's door. "I'm outta here," Kathleen said, as she entered. "Do you need anything before I go?"

"Nope." Diamond spoke without looking up. "Close the door on your way out." She knew Kathleen still stood there, could envision the look of motherly concern on her face. Her frustration caused her to speak more sharply than she intended. "I'm fine, Kat. See you tomorrow."

There was silence for a moment and then she said, "Bye, Diamond." A soft click of the door punctuated Kathleen's departure.

Diamond sighed, even as Jackson's voice invaded her conscience: *Black American princess.* She knew that right now her actions were those of exactly that, a spoiled diva. Kathleen was the last person who deserved such treatment. But she was still too much in sulk mode to dismiss her assistant getting all up in her business—sanely translated—showing genuine concern. *At least she's gone and I can mope in private.* But, no; Kathleen was obviously a glutton for punishment because less than a minute later the click of the doorknob signaled her return.

*Okay, I've had it.* Steaming, Diamond whirled around. "What is it now? Oh, hey, Dex."

A slight smirk accompanied Dexter into the room. "Hey, sis." He walked over and sat in the chair across from Diamond's desk.

Diamond never looked up. "I'm busy, so whatever it is, make it quick."

Dexter leaned over, snatched what she was reading out of her hands and laughed at her glowering countenance like he was twelve.

"I mean it, Dexter." Oh, she was really serious now, full name used and all. "I'm trying to get out of here."

Dexter placed the paper back down. "Hot date tonight?"

Diamond huffed, glared at Dexter and returned to her reading, hoping he'd get the don't-mess-with-me-'cause-I'm-not-in-the-mood message. "Bye, brother."

He didn't. Rather, he kept sitting there, staring, a stupid I've-got-a-secret look on his face. Diamond didn't even care what that was about. But she was getting ready to find out.

"Or was that date this afternoon?"

Had everybody on the premises been drinking nosy water? Not four hours away from her first dalliance in a year and suddenly everyone was interested in her dating schedule and mental status. That "everyone" at this point included only Kathleen and Dexter was beside the point. Two people in her business were two people too many. Diamond stopped looking at the report she'd been holding but not reading the past ten minutes and tried to keep her cool by adopting a nonchalant attitude. "Ha-ha. My brother's got jokes. You must have seen Jackson by my offices earlier. He owns the construction company that is doing our renovation, or have you forgotten that minor detail?" She waited. The smirk remained on Dexter's face. "It was business."

Dexter's eyes stayed locked on hers. The smirk stayed, too. "Uh-huh."

"Whatever." Diamond was proud of how apparently bored she must look. The disguise took effort.

"You're going to sit there and tell me that nothing happened between you and Jackson when you took him on a tour of the vineyard?"

*So he's talked to Daddy. Either that or he saw Jackson leaving the warehouse.* "That got interrupted. Jackson received a phone call from his assistant. Emergency. Had to dash back to his office."

"That may be true, but he didn't leave too quickly."

Diamond shrugged. "I don't know how he left. I stayed behind to check out the inventory."

Dexter laughed. "You checked out more than wine." He reached into his pocket. "I admit to my share of dallying, but—" flicking his wrist, he tossed something on Diamond's desk "—this ain't mine."

The reflection of the gold foil on Diamond's varnished desktop shone like a thousand suns.

"What's that?" she asked, her casual attitude slipping a notch.

"If we were in court, I'd call it admissible evidence," Dexter said, stretching his legs out in front of him.

"And I'd argue reasonable doubt." Diamond willed herself not to blush as she flicked the "evidence" off her desk. "Not to mention that you're nasty…picking up an anonymous condom wrapper. A dozen people are in and out of that cellar. It could belong to any of them."

"Uh-huh." Dexter continued to eye his sister. "But the way you're over there squirming, I'd say I'm closer to the truth."

"What you're closer to is getting kicked out of my office. Shouldn't you be focused on your own love life, hanging out with your Latin flavor and whatnot?"

"Besides," Dexter continued, ignoring Diamond's attempt to shift the focus, "I was down at the site earlier and talked to some of the men. One of them saw you showing Jackson around. The rumor mill is hopping, sister."

"Just make sure you don't add to it, brother. My interest in Jackson ends at the construction site."

"Maybe," Dexter said, rising from the chair and heading to the door. "But is that all that Jackson wants?"

Diamond waited until her brother had closed the door and then leaned back heavily against the chair. The truth of the matter was Diamond had no idea what Jackson wanted. And from the hurried way he left after they'd made love, she deduced that when it came to anything outside of the workplace, maybe the cocky, arrogant love machine that still had her throbbing had already gotten what he came for.

# Chapter 16

Jackson placed his hands on either side of the marble shower and let the six powerful shower jets hit him from all sides. Abe's interrogation—because to call it a discussion would be putting it too mildly—had been grueling but necessary. It had been years since Jackson had opened up about his less than humble beginnings, the start in life that he swore to put behind him the moment he left South Central and landed in San Diego's tony suburb of La Jolla. He'd hoped—prayed even—that the severing from his childhood could be clean and complete. A part of him, however, knew that there was no total escape from the ties that bound him. Family was family, and blood was thicker than concrete.

Moving his head from side to side, he let the water run over his close-cropped curls and tried to work out the kinks in his neck. Mental pictures from another meeting, the one that had happened before Abe's pointed questioning, came to mind. He instantly hardened and was reminded that the

break-in and letter weren't the only things that had Jackson
tight. After Abe left, he'd tried to reach Diamond. Her assistant had told him that she was unavailable. He could just
about guess what that meant. She was pissed and didn't want
to talk. He'd be the first to admit that his exit was whack.
But she needed to know that the extenuating circumstances
made his quick getaway necessary.

Cutting off the water, he stepped from the shower and,
after wrapping a towel around his waist, he reached for his
phone. There was one text: from Marissa. She'd been able
to locate Diamond's personal number. He opened it up and
smiled for the first time since he and Diamond made love.
Seconds later, he tapped the number that Marissa had sent
him, and seconds after that, he heard the voice that made
things beat faster and get harder. "Hello, Diamond. It's Jackson."

The intake of breath on the other end of the phone was audible. "Jackson! How did you get my cell number?"

"That's one thing you need to learn about me, baby girl. I
always get what I want."

The next evening, Jackson and Diamond sat at a restaurant
located midway between Temecula and San Diego. It was a
Friday night, and as such, the place was fairly crowded. But
Jackson had finagled a corner booth for them and then sat
down beside Diamond instead of opposite her.

"Thanks for coming," he said after they'd placed drink
orders.

"You left me little choice," Diamond replied, trying without success to keep the pout out of her voice.

"Spoiled brat," Jackson mumbled.

"What did you say?"

"I said sorry about that." And he managed to keep a
straight face while doing so. "But I knew that you'd come

kicking and screaming, even with the threat of telling your dad about our little tryst."

"Yeah, well, it may be too late to keep a lid on it anyway." Diamond told Jackson about Dexter's find. "I came because we need to talk. What happened was a one-time lapse in judgment. It won't happen again."

Jackson shrugged. The sooner the world knew that he and Diamond had a thing going, the better. As for what they had being over, he figured that for now he'd let her hang on to that illusion. "Here." He held out a box.

"What's this?"

"A peace offering. Open it."

She did and couldn't help laughing at what was inside. "A diamond-covered rooster brooch, Jackson. Really?"

"A rooster is one word for it. But others call it a cock."

Diamond laughed in spite of herself. "How romantic," she drily finished.

"Just wanted to give you something to remember me by."

She looked at this arrogant, cocky guy, caught the hint of vulnerability and longing for acceptance shining in those dark eyes. He put up a good front, but Diamond knew this gift was a bigger deal than Jackson was making of it. "Okay, it's gawdy but kinda cute." She began pinning it to her designer tee.

"Here, let me."

Okay, pinning a rooster on someone's shirt should not be romantic, but it was. Diamond breathed in Jackson's fresh, woodsy scent, felt the heat from his fingers as they brushed against her skin. If she turned her face to the right, just a bit, their lips would be in dangerously close proximity to each other, and if she placed her right hand just above the thigh just inches away, then, well, she could squeeze his rooster.

Their drinks arrived. Diamond quickly reached for hers and, after a sip, stirred around the amber-colored liquid with the maraschino cherry that perched on top. "Why'd you have to leave?" she said, in a Herculean effort to force her thoughts away from farm animals.

"Problems at the office." *And that's putting it mildly.*

Sounded like the perfect answer…for one hiding a female. "Are you going to give me details, or is this classified information?"

"It's classified."

Never long on patience, Diamond quickly found herself bored with Jackson's word games. But his vagueness was welcomed; it was what she needed to stay clear on what was happening here—a big, fat nothing. "Well, since I seem to be the only one with new information, here it is. From this day forward, ours will be a business-only relationship. You are to conduct yourself accordingly. We have to work together for the next few weeks, after which it will be perfectly okay if I never see you again. Now, since we've cleared the air, I'll be leaving. I've better things to do on a Friday night—"

"Like what?"

"Like none of your business." Diamond would swallow her tongue before she'd release the fact that a night of novel reading was the exciting item on her agenda. She took another sip of her drink, piercing Jackson with her gaze.

"You're right, Diamond, you deserve an explanation on why I had to leave so quickly. But that's only one of the reasons I asked you here. The other reason is this—what happened yesterday was amazing. I've had my share of lovers, but I've never felt the way I did yesterday afternoon."

"And how was that?" Diamond queried, chiding herself for doing so while hiding her surprise—and her feelings—behind sarcasm.

Jackson leaned forward, took Diamond's small hands into his much larger ones. "It felt like magic. When I was inside you, baby, it was like coming home. I know you said wha happened was a one-time fling, but for the record, I want to hang out with you for a minute."

"How long is a minute?" Diamond asked.

Jackson shrugged. "Until we're both satisfied or…whatever."

Diamond sat back and gazed at the man in front of her. Yet again, she was seeing a side of Jackson that she hadn't seen before. This one was honest and tender and looked finer than anyone had a right to in just a simple, pale yellow button-down shirt. The familiar heat in her core began uncoiling. Diamond looked away. "I felt the same way about what happened. It was different." She looked at him. "Special. But no matter how good the sex, Jackson, and it was amazing, I'm looking for more in my life—permanence, commitment. And that's not you."

Inwardly, Jackson flinched. She'd mentioned commitment, but that's not what he heard. His translation? That a man like him—former wannabe gangbanger and drug dealer and all-around ghetto child—wasn't good enough for a princess. But on the outside? Cool as the proverbial green summer vegetable. In spite of this, he pressed her. "You don't even know me."

"Yes, but I've heard about you, and the story is that you're a ladies' man."

"I've never led a woman on. Everything that has gone down in my love life has been by mutual consent."

"Perhaps, but mutual consent doesn't always cancel out a broken heart." Now, Diamond deduced, it was her turn to be honest. "I don't know if I could keep my feelings casual where you're concerned, but one thing I know for sure is I'm not willing to spend my time with a Casanova and spin my wheels in a going-nowhere affair."

Jackson slowly nodded. "Fair enough."

Diamond realized there was much more to this man than

met the eye or made the paper. For all the news about Jackson Wright she'd gleaned from her brothers, there was little known beyond his professional acumen and carefree, playboy ways. An uncomfortable feeling came over her as she acknowledged this truth: she wanted to know more, and she wanted to "fling" at least one more time.

# Chapter 17

Diamond sat back and looked around, for the first time noticing the candle-holding hollowed pumpkins that graced the tables and announced Halloween. "What happened at your company yesterday?"

"I thought you had to leave."

She made a show of looking at her watch. "I have some time."

Jackson leaned toward her. "Can you keep a confidence?" His voice was low, his breath wet against her earlobe.

Diamond nodded, swallowed.

"Promise?"

"Yes."

"There was a break-in at my office."

Diamond's brow knitted in confusion and concern. "What would someone want so badly from you that they'd steal to get it?"

Jackson shifted in his seat and took a drink. This wasn't

going to be as easy as he thought. There was no way he could tell her that the person broke into his office to *leave* something. "I've got some people looking into it. What can I say?" Jackson said with a shrug, his voice as casual as if he were discussing basketball scores. "Everyone isn't happy with my success."

"You have enemies?"

"No doubt."

Diamond smiled. "What successful person doesn't have a hater or two?"

Jackson's mind went to who he believed was his number-one nemesis: Solomon Dent. Solomon had been John Wright's right-hand man, the man who thought himself a shoo-in for the position that Jackson now occupied. John had included Solomon in his will, had stipulated that he be president for a period of five years before turning over the reins to his nephew, but for Solomon, a little piece of the pie wasn't enough. He'd wanted it all. After a vicious court battle, Jackson prevailed. Solomon was awarded a substantial financial settlement. But the job hadn't been just about money but also prestige. A man with his ego could still be smarting over the early, forced departure. The fact that it was self-inflicted seemed to have been lost in translation.

And there were others rivals: both from his professional and private life, including a man who blamed Jackson for his ex-fiancée's alienated affections. The truth was the junior architect had fallen in love with Jackson. But he hadn't returned her affections. Even when she'd shown up buck naked on his doorstep, save for a sarong, he'd turned her down. But to hear old boy tell it, Jackson had pulled her kicking and screaming from the brother's arms. More than one person had overheard the threats of what this man wanted to do if he ever caught Jackson late at night in a dark alley. And after today's note he'd acknowledged another possibility, one that seemed far-reaching at best: that someone from his childhood thought he'd talked out of school and, now, more than a decade since he'd moved from the hood, was attempting retribution.

The waitress came and took their orders. Once she'd left the table, Jackson asked, "Have you eaten here before?"

Diamond nodded, working hard to keep a neutral expression on her face.

She was only partly successful. Jackson couldn't tell what lay under the flash of darkness that appeared in her eyes. Hurt? Anger? Disappointment? "Bad memories?"

"Something like that" was her vague response. "But the food is good."

"It's nothing compared to the dessert I have in mind."

The dark look of desire in Jackson's eyes was unmistakable. Diamond placed a hand on her stomach to try and still the butterflies that gathered there. Fat chance. She wanted this man with a vengeance, which was the very reason why, as much as she wanted to, she really shouldn't be intimate again. If she was this turned out after one good sexing, what would she be like after a second round? A candidate for Dr. Drew is what, she decided, working with the good doctor to cure an addiction of the Jackson kind.

"Diamond Drake," Jackson murmured. "Where'd you get that name?"

Diamond smiled. "My father. Unlike most men who want sons, Dad always wanted a little girl. When I arrived, he deemed me his jewel and named me after one that was beautiful yet resilient."

"And humble, too."

"Those are my dad's words, not mine." Diamond arched a brow. "Do you disagree with my father?" The look on Jackson's face brought instant moisture between her legs.

"Do I look like I disagree with him? Baby, you're as fine as Drake wine in the summertime."

"Ha! That sounds like a line my dad would use!"

"I don't doubt it, especially since it came from the arsenal of sayings Uncle John used on Aunt Evie."

For the first time since meeting, the two experienced a casual camaraderie, and Diamond's smile was genuine as she looked across the table at a man she already adored. "Tell me about your—"

A couple entering the dining room stopped Diamond mid-speak.

"Who is it?" Jackson asked without turning around.

*Of all the restaurants and of all the nights, what are the chances?* Diamond wasn't able to keep the frown off her face as she answered, "You're getting ready to come face-to-face with my bad memory." She looked up as the couple approached their table. Benjamin Carter was as handsome as she remembered: a bald-headed chocolate drop who made up in length what he lacked in height. Until this afternoon, she'd thought his was the appendages of appendages. But now she knew better. *Thank, God.* The woman beside him could have been Diamond's cousin, so much did they look alike. Similar height, weight, complexion and, had Diamond not recently cut hers, shoulder-length hair. Yep, definitely could have been the Bobbsey Twins.

"Hello, Diamond."

Diamond nodded. "Benjamin."

You could cut the tension with a Q-tip.

"I just wanted to say a quick hello. How's the family?"

"Fine," Diamond answered Benjamin but eyed her twin.

"Hello," the woman said—smile sincere, hand outstretched. "I'm Pat, Benjamin's wife."

*Hold on. Back up. Did she say "wife"?* Diamond summoned up an act that was Oscar-worthy. Her expression remained so blank you would have sworn she'd shot Botox. She shook Pat's hand. "Diamond Drake."

A flash of recognition appeared, but Pat was going for an Emmy herself. "It's a pleasure to meet you."

"And this," Diamond said while casually placing a hand on his thigh as if it were the most natural thing to do, "is Jackson Wright." She leaned into him as she added, "Baby, this is my ex I told you about. The one I dumped...remember?"

*Oh, snap.* Those words shot out so fast that even sprinter Usain Bolt couldn't have caught them. Grandma Mary would not have been pleased, but a residual of hurt that Diamond thought dead and buried had resurrected and pushed class and decorum right out of the way. She clamped her mouth shut, but the horse was not only out of the barn...it could run straight into Pat's mouth, which hung wide open. "I'm sorry," she said. "That wasn't nice."

"No, it wasn't, but that's your nature," Benjamin retorted. "Which is why I dumped *you*. Come on, Pat," he said, reaching for his wife's hand. "Let's join our more civilized company." A slightly bewildered-looking Pat followed her husband, Diamond's snort her only goodbye. The departing couple almost bumped into the waitress, who was delivering salads to Jackson and Diamond's table.

Jackson waited until the waitress had left. "So," he murmured, running a finger up Diamond's arm. Her shiver of a response brought a smile. "Do you want to tell your *baby* what that was all about?"

Her desire for Jackson had pierced through the anger, but Diamond still reached for her purse. "I'm leaving." Benjamin and Pat had been seated a distance away, but right now Yankee Stadium would have been too small a common room for her and her ex.

Jackson placed a staying hand on Diamond's arm. "Baby, wait. We've not yet eaten."

"I've lost my appetite."

## Chapter 18

After tossing several bills on the table, Jackson rushed after the ball of fire that was his date. "Diamond, wait!"

She increased her stride, not wanting Jackson to see how badly Benjamin's unexpected news had upset her. When had he gotten married? And how had he done so without her finding out? She reached her car, but when it came to long strides, five foot nine was no match for six foot five. Jackson had gotten there one step ahead of her and now placed his hand on the door.

"Give me your keys," he demanded.

"Why?" Diamond angrily brushed what she swore was the last tear she'd cry over men from her cheek.

"Because I don't want you driving upset." Jackson held out his hand, with a don't-you-dare-try-me look in his eyes.

"I'm not upset," she said, cursing another tear that dared to fall. Jackson crossed his arms and leaned against Diamond's car. After a brief glare down, she gave him the keys. "So now you're going to drive two cars," she said with all the dryness of the Mojave Desert. "This I've got to see."

Jackson reached for her hand. "I'll bring you back to your car later, but right now, you're coming with me."

"Where are we going?"

"My place."

"Uh, I don't think so."

"I didn't ask what you thought. That was a statement, not a question. Now, I can either pick you up or you can walk on your own, but either way you're not going to be alone right now. You're coming with me."

Diamond took Jackson's hand, and together they walked to his Maserati. She immediately recognized the white BMW beside it. She'd been with Benjamin when he purchased it— two months before she'd pressed him to set a wedding date and he'd flat out refused. And now he was married? Again, the tears threatened, and Diamond realized that Jackson had been right. This was no time for her to be alone.

Jackson's sports car ate up the distance between the restaurant and his home. After keying in the code, a large wrought-iron gate opened, and Diamond felt as though she'd been transported to the Mediterranean. Strategically placed lights emphasized the large home's majesty, its pale-salmon coating a stark contrast to the black night sky. Its various levels and angles were architecturally sophisticated, and the turret at the back of the building added to the mansion's overall charm.

Diamond, who'd grown up in the lap of luxury and whose ten-thousand-square-foot estate was no small potatoes, was impressed. From what she could see, the grounds were as stunning as the building, but there was more—something indefinable—about Jackson's surroundings. The place felt like a fortress, no, a sanctuary. That was it. As soon as they'd entered the gates, Diamond felt protected beyond the ordinary. Her shoulders lowered as she visibly relaxed and whispered, "This is amazing." It seemed as if to speak louder would break some type of magical spell.

Jackson smiled, appreciative of Diamond's obvious good taste. "Thank you, baby. It's called *Cielo*...my little slice of heaven."

"Heaven...that's what *cielo* means?"

Jackson nodded. Following his uncle's and aunt's deaths, Jackson had thought of moving into their place, but the memories were too great and painful. So he'd sold their home and all its contents and built the oceanfront dwelling of his dreams from the ground up. It was also during this time that he changed the company name: from Wright Works to Boss Construction.

"It's beautiful, Jackson."

Bypassing the five-car garage, Jackson navigated the circular drive until they reached the home's front door. He turned off the engine, then leaned over and placed a gentle kiss on Diamond's cheek. "Wait here."

Diamond watched as he exited the car, curious as to his intentions. She soon found out. Jackson bounded around to her side of the car and opened her door. "M'lady," he said with a bow.

Diamond smiled, suddenly feeling like a teenybopper on her first date. She held out her hand. "M'lord."

Jackson kissed her hand before tucking it in the crook of his arm. "Welcome to my home. *Mi casa es su casa.*"

They went inside. In a glance, Diamond took in the two-story ceiling, generous foyer, sparkling crystal chandelier and a double winding staircase that seemed straight out of a fairy tale. Her heels clicked against the smooth marble flooring as she followed Jackson into a formal living room. Luxury with a capital *L* oozed from every nook and cranny, and while the trappings were undoubtedly expensive, a homeyness somehow exuded, the kind that made you want to take off your shoes and stay awhile.

Jackson gave Diamond's hand a final squeeze. "Make yourself at home." Diamond observed his long, sure strides as he crossed the floor to the fireplace. After placing a few pieces of kindling on top of the larger logs already arranged, he pushed a button and within seconds a fire blazed in the hearth.

"Real wood," Diamond said, as she continued to walk around and admire the room. "I like that."

Jackson's eyes narrowed as purposeful strides ate up the distance between them. "And I like this."

Diamond closed her eyes for the kiss but instead felt strong, protective arms wrap themselves around her. For a moment, they simply stood there, feeling each others' rapid heartbeat, breathing in a combination of woodsy and floral scents. Diamond could feel heat, but she wasn't sure whether it emanated from his body or hers. The wetness? It was definitely her. She brought her arms to Jackson's back, reveling in the broad expanse of manliness she felt there. His hands traveled, too, and soon they were kneading her shoulders.

"You're so tight."

Diamond rested her head against his shoulder and enjoyed his ministrations. "That feels good."

He kissed her temple.

*So does that.*

And the top of her head.

*And that. Just a kiss,* she reminded herself. *That's all. Nothing more can happen.*

Then he nipped her ear before sucking the lobe into his mouth, and Diamond got the distinct feeling that she'd be picking her car up in the morning.

# Chapter 19

Diamond tightened her grip around Jackson's waist—and just in time. Because Jackson lifted her head and claimed her mouth in a kiss so hot that she needed something to hold on to lest she keel straight over. His long, thick tongue sought and found territory unclaimed in the previous meeting. He massaged her head, neck and shoulders, his tongue massaging the inside of her mouth. Intending to take full advantage of the one-kiss-that's-all-and-nothing-else-can-happen moment Diamond shifted her head for better access, skimming her fingers along the small of his back before resting her hand on his firm, round butt. Her nipples hardened, begged for attention; her kitty throbbed intensely. If possible, she knew it would have audibly meowed. She broke the kiss, looked deep into Jackson's eyes and was sure she conveyed this message *sorry, I can't be with you again.* Her telepathic signals must have been off because he promptly took her hand and headed to those beautiful double wrought-iron fixtures that Diamond would later dub the stairway to heaven.

Also later, Diamond would take her time and admire the ample landing, loft-style sitting room and bedrooms located on both sides of the hallway. Now she fixed her eyes on their obvious destination: a set of double doors at the end of the hall. *Time to put on the breaks, Diamond. Speak now or forever hold your peace!* Jackson opened the door. Diamond stifled a gasp. At any moment, she expected to see a choir of angels because this sure looked like paradise. Diamond eyed the custom-made king-size bed that rested on a large platform of cherry wood. It beckoned, but Jackson kept walking past the walk-in closet to another door that opened into the en suite bathroom. But really, that was too tame a word. This room was a virtual spa, complete with sauna, bidet and vessel sinks amid sparkling glass, hand-carved stone and a plant-filled water feature. A massive skylight revealed a scenic expanse of twinkling stars.

"Take off your clothes," Jackson commanded, his voice low and husky. "I want to see you naked."

Was she a dim-witted robot acting on command? Why was she reaching for the hem of her sleeveless tee and pulling it over her head when she should be saying, Thank you very much but could you please take me home? Jackson deftly unbuttoned and unzipped her jeans, kissing her stomach and thighs as he helped rid her of them. *Oh, that's why.* He watched as she unfastened her bra. It hit the ground. Her thong joined it.

"Better?" Diamond asked, her grin devilish and saucy.

"Indeed." Jackson's eyes never left Diamond's as he quickly unbuttoned his shirt, pulled off his T-shirt and removed his slacks.

Mr. Happy swayed from side to side like a massive pendulum. Two more seconds of staring and Diamond may have been hypnotized. But she had better ideas for that work of art. All afternoon she'd thought of how it would taste in her mouth. This was right after the thoughts that they'd never be together again. She took a step, wrapped her fingers around his magic shaft and noted that her fingers could not touch. *Day-um!* Had it grown some more? She licked her lips and bent her head…

"No, not yet," Jackson whispered. He moved away, and Diamond felt as bereft as Tom Hanks in *Castaway,* as if she were floating on a single plank in the midst of an ocean and her volleyball had suddenly floated away.

"Come here."

She walked to the tub. She looked down into a mass of tiny bubbles, surprised because she hadn't seen him pour bubble bath.

"Get in."

The silkiness of Jackson's voice made further questions unnecessary. At this point, Jackson could have told her to paddle a blow-up raft to Catalina Island, and if he was the promise on the other side, she would have been a rowing sister. She sat down in the midst of the bubbles, and right away it was as if a thousand tiny fingers were massaging her skin; from head to toe, she felt the sensations. She closed her eyes and let out an audible sigh. Now there was no doubt. This was heaven.

After a moment, she felt a touch on her arm. Jackson directed her forward and then slipped in behind her. He pulled her back against his chest, wrapped his arms around her and, for a moment, they simply enjoyed the bliss of design's next level from the Jacuzzi…the bubble massage. His hands began to roam her body. Diamond's legs immediately parted in silent invitation. He chuckled, and she would have felt chagrin had it not been for the fact that instead of her nana it was her nipples he wanted. He tweaked one and then the other as he placed feathery kisses along her neck. While still rolling a springy nub between his fingers, he took the other hand and found Diamond's treasure. He slid a finger along her silky folds, and Diamond almost exploded right then. She spread her legs, but he continued to tease—barely rubbing her nub with the tip of his finger, while increasing the pressure on her achy breast. The feeling of his hands on her skin and the stimulating bubbles was ecstasy enough, but then, without warning, he buried his tongue in her ear and his finger inside her. Diamond cried out in surprise at the spasm that signaled the first of several orgasms she would have this night.

Before she could stop trembling, Jackson stepped out of the tub, lifted her into his arms and strode into the bedroom. Without thought of value, he laid her still-wet body on top of the raw silk comforter and climbed onto the bed. He stared at her, and Diamond's body reacted to his fervent gaze. Incredibly, though she'd just experienced release, her nipples hardened and her muscles tightened. Would she ever get enough of this guy?

Obviously Jackson didn't think so. Because after a few seconds of lightly running his fingers all over her body, he whispered a simple command: "Spread your legs."

Diamond obeyed.

"Wider."

Diamond swallowed, closed her eyes and followed instructions. There was an excruciating moment where nothing happened, and she imagined Jackson staring down at her. This turned her on even more. Then she felt a burst of air on her exposed flesh, followed by quick, short licks of tongue. She moaned and blindly reached for his head, wanting—no, *needing*—to feel the pressure of him flush against her, inside her, everywhere. He complied, lapping, nibbling, tasting her over and again. Diamond relished the assault, but figuring what was good for the goose was equally so for the gander, she rolled over, got on her knees and issued a command of her own. "Lie back."

Jackson's obedience was accompanied by a slow, easy smile. He put his hands behind his head, watching Diamond's every move. She clasped his ample manhood, massaged it from base to tip. She ran a thumbnail along his sac. He hissed. Now it was Diamond's turn for the knowing chuckle. *Ah, yes.* Wetting her lips, she leaned down and kissed the tip before taking in as much of him as possible. She used her tongue to worship at his sizable shrine, following the path of his vein like a GPS, caressing his shaft as if it were a Smithsonian contender. She took him into her mouth and sucked. Hard. Jackson's intake of breath was immediate, followed by a deep moan.

Oh, oh. Playtime was over, and Jackson was now in command. He reached for a condom and shielded himself. He lifted her to her knees, got behind her and, after using his tongue in ways that Diamond could only have imagined, poised himself for entry. He made them one with a single body-tingling, mind-boggling powerful stroke. Up. Down. In. Out. Oh…so…slowly. His thrusts were powerful, purposeful, as if to brand her very soul. Diamond grabbed fistfuls of comforter, matching him thrust for vigorous thrust. They loved, then slept and loved some more. And as streaks of orange and purple announced the dawn, Jackson was loving her still.

## Chapter 20

Monday morning arrived, and Diamond was as chipper as the birds that trilled outside her bedroom window. She'd spent the weekend with Jackson, not picking up her car from the restaurant until last night, after Jackson begrudgingly drove her away from their lair of love. Unable to keep her mind on work—or anything else but Jackson for the past seventy-two hours—she rose from her desk and walked to the window. Yes, indeed, today was a beautiful day.

A light tap and then Kathleen stepped into Diamond's office. "Good morning, Diamond. You're here early." Diamond turned, Kathleen took in the glow on her face, and the mother of five immediately knew how it had gotten there. Heck, the late, great Ray Charles could have seen the glow. The astronauts parked at the moon's space station could have seen that glow. "Enjoy your weekend?"

"It was okay," Diamond said, trying for a tone of major disinterest.

She was trying so hard that Kathleen almost suggested adding a yawn for effect.

Diamond returned to her desk. "How was yours?"

"Oh, the usual. Sex all weekend—swinging from chandeliers, hitting high notes, just another forty-eight in the Fitzgerald household." Diamond smirked. "Okay, since you want the PG version, I went with Carol and the grands to Old Town—costumes, haunted houses, too much candy, the works."

"You didn't dress up."

Kathleen looked genuinely chagrined. "Why, of course I did, me lady. Dressed up as an Irish maid, I did," she announced in a respectable brogue. "Then went home and showed Bernie my lucky charms."

"Ha!"

"But we were both too tired to do much more than look."

Both ladies laughed and then got down to Drake Wines business. "Oh, one more thing," Diamond said, wrapping up. "I have a meeting with Jackson Wright at two."

"Another one?" Kathleen asked innocently. "He was just here on Thursday."

Diamond knew Kathleen was fishing, but she didn't take the bait. "Yes, and with the expedited schedule, we'll probably be joined at the hip for the next two weeks." Diamond thought of ways they'd been joined last weekend and felt herself grow warm. "That's it, Kat. Please hold my calls for the next hour."

A crush of meetings and an hour-long phone call with the writer doing the *O Magazine* story helped time fly by. Before she knew it, two o'clock arrived. It had been less than twenty-four hours since his scorching kiss in the restaurant parking lot, but her stomach flip-flopped at the thought of seeing Jackson. He made her feel all gooey and girly inside, and today she'd swapped her more businesslike attire for decidedly feminine look. When Kathleen announced his arrival, Diamond made one final adjustment to her apparel, quickly checked herself in the mirror and was out the door.

"You look good enough to eat," Jackson said once they were buckled in the cart and heading toward the grapevines. *And you bless a pair of jeans like nobody's business.* "I'm at work, and the trees have eyes. Behave."

Jackson admired her openly. "You smell good. And I like the dress. What color would you call that…pink? Rose?"

"It contains both," Diamond answered, warmed by the flattery. Flattery would indeed get Jackson everywhere he'd already been.

"I like it."

"Thanks."

There was a companionable silence and then he said, "Did your parents mention anything about us?"

"No, but Mom called to tell me what time dinner was being served and to make sure I'd be there."

"Dex talked?"

"I don't know. But even if he didn't, my mom could make money on a psychic hotline. 'Staying with friends,'" Diamond said, making air quotes, "doesn't exactly qualify as an explanation for a weekend away from the Drake Estate."

"But you're a grown woman. She keeps tabs on you like that?"

"Not exactly. But my staying out all weekend is unusual behavior." Actually, *unheard of* would have been a better description. The two other dates she'd had since being dumped by Benjamin had been most forgettable, a fact that she hadn't withheld from the household. So the fact that she'd spent the weekend out and on news of such was as quiet as a church mouse…well…that was something that wouldn't get by Mrs. Genevieve Drake—not on any day of the week.

They reached the easternmost tip of the vine field, and

away from work and prying eyes, Diamond removed the short-waist white jacket, revealing her halter dress beneath. Jackson immediately took advantage and placed a soft, wet kiss on her bare shoulder.

"Do I have to wear this jacket and bake in the heat? Or will you act right?"

"Baby," he said, eyeing her behind and licking his lips, "I *am* acting right."

Diamond ignored him. "In the journey of wine from grape to glass," she said as if narrating a PBS special, "this—" making a sweeping motion across the mass acreage "—is where it all begins. The plots are sectioned off by type of grape—barbera, cabernet franc, cabernet sauvignon, sauvignon blanc, chardonnay, chenin blanc and merlot." Jackson ran a finger down her arm. She swatted it away. "We also grow a few lesser known or less popular varieties such as pinot noir and its clone, pinot gris, Grenache, Shiraz, Viognier and Zinfandel."

They walked down a row where plump, dark grape clusters swung from the vine. Jackson stopped. "Which grape is this?"

"That's the Nebbiolo," Diamond said. "Like you, a bad boy." Jackson's brow cocked in question. "Notoriously hard to grow and tame. Along with tannic and tarry qualities, it has a chocolaty taste."

"Hum, like me indeed." Diamond swatted his shoulder. "So now you think I'm vain, huh?"

"I prefer *cocky*." Too late Diamond realized the double entendre.

"I know you do," Jackson said, his smile rivaling the sun that shone overhead. "You *preferred* it all weekend long."

"Whatever." Though the sudden reddened hue of Diamond's skin showed that she knew exactly of what he spoke.

Jackson rubbed his finger across the grape's firm skin. "Can I eat one?"

"Sure." Diamond reached into her pocket and pulled out a type of Swiss knife. "Here, let me." She snipped off a small cluster. "I have water in the cart."

"What do you have to do…wash off the insecticides and pesticides you spray on this crop?"

"Our wines are organic, thank you very much. We use only natural pesticides to keep the bugs away. This is just to remove the dirt."

Jackson popped a grape into his mouth. "God made dirt, so dirt don't hurt."

Diamond laughed. She hadn't heard that saying since grade school. "You're silly."

"Or there's another one…what's a little dirt among friends. Baby, these are sweet. Here, taste one." Diamond reached for the grape, but Jackson pulled back. "Open that sweet mouth of yours." She did, and when taking the grape, Diamond's lips brushed against Jackson's fingers. Just like that, the smoldering sparks became flames.

"I'm hot, too," Jackson said, pulling the shirt he wore over his head to reveal hard, rippling muscles.

Diamond could stare at his chest all day and never get enough. She could do many things with Jackson all day and never get enough. Even his tattoo wasn't a deterrent. Normally, Diamond didn't like them, but on him it was one of the sexiest things she'd ever seen, especially when outlining it with her tongue.

"Here, have another one."

Jackson placed the grape between his teeth and leaned forward. It was probably a futile battle to resist him, not to mention a day late and a dollar short; nonetheless, she played hard to get. She pulled a grape from the cluster in his hand and plopped it into her mouth. "Delicious."

"Really? Let me taste it."

And before she could protest further, there was chest against breast and tongue in mouth. The taste of grapes mixed with desire was a potent combination, and as crazy as the notion was, Diamond wanted to be taken there, on the spot, between two rows of "bad boy" grapes. Fortunately, there were one or two vestiges of sanity left, and she used them to form her next five words: "Let's go to Papa Dee's."

## Chapter 21

Diamond walked to the cart with Jackson right on her heels. "Papa who?"

"Dee," she replied over her shoulder. "Short for David." She jumped into the cart, started it and was off milliseconds after Jackson's heel left the dirt.

"Dang, girl. Slow down!"

Diamond went on as if she were having tea in the garden instead of driving a cart forty miles an hour over gravel. "David Drake Sr. is my great-grandfather. He was born in that house on the hill. I'll show you the room. My great-great-grandfather Nicodemus built this place…well, him and his worker friends, with their bare hands." Diamond hit a rut. The cart rose a foot off the ground and came down with a thud. "Whoa! Sorry."

Jackson was busy leaving finger imprints on the dash through a Jaws of Life-style clutch. He shot a fierce scowl at Diamond. "Slow down!"

"Ha!" Diamond pressed her foot on the gas and went from grass to gravel on two wheels. "Spoken by the person who drives a Maserati. Cute."

They reached the house on the hill, a two-story, square-shaped number with a red hipped roof. Compared to the Drake Estate, one would describe it as humble; yet there was a majestic quality to it, an unmistakable air of importance that emanated from the worn planks of wood. Jackson and Diamond exited the cart, their conversation muted by the energy around them.

Jackson walked up to the side of the house that was facing them and looked into the window. He ran his hand along the pane and noted the pristine workmanship still evident a hundred years after completion. It was as if he could sense the worth of the men who'd built it, imagined their camaraderie while working together, mixed with determination and pride. "Good work," he said.

Diamond joined him at the window. "The entrance is around here," she said, her voice low, reverent. "It's locked, but there's a secret hiding place for the key. You have to promise not to tell anyone where it is."

Jackson looked chagrined. "Who would I tell?"

Diamond's smile was soft, unreadable. "Come on."

They walked around to the side of the house where a porch that spanned the length of the house had seen better days. There were three short steps to the door. Jackson bypassed those and stepped directly onto the porch's wooden planks. They creaked under his weight. Diamond walked to the edge of the porch, lifted one of the planks and retrieved a large, old heavy key. The lock protested, but eventually the knob turned and the couple went inside. Jackson's eyes filled with wonder as he noted the excellent craftsmanship of the wooden floors, beveled windows and pressed brick fireplace. Built-in bookcases framed the fireplace, and the dining room was beamed and Dutch-paneled, with a heavy plate rail and buffet spanning the back wall. Faded floral wallpaper suggested a woman's touch. The whole place reeked with the Obama mantra: Yes, we can.

Jackson asked, "How'd your family get this land?"

"My great-great-grandfather Nicodemus was part Creole, from New Orleans, and came here with his owner in the late 1800s. He and Pierre Drake, his owner, had grown up together and were more like brothers than master and slave. When they made the trip west to expand the Drake family fortunes, Pierre almost died. But Nicodemus's mother, Henriette, was trained in the healing arts. She passed her knowledge of herbs and other natural ingredients as remedies on to her children. Aside from having a magical way with animals, Nicodemus was what was called back then a root doctor. He saved Pierre's life. The family was so grateful that they promised to will part of the land to him, and when Pierre died, that's exactly what happened."

"That's an amazing story, Diamond. And such a rarity— people of color owning so much land."

"That hasn't come without its struggles," Diamond admitted. "More than once, various entities have tried to steal this rich property. But the Drakes were smart people, and their will was ironclad. It also hasn't hurt that we've remained in contact with our White counterparts and attend their family reunion every year."

"Your ancestor's former owners?"

Diamond nodded. "When the last lawsuit came, trying to take the land from Papa Dee, it was Pierre's great-great-grandson, now a lawyer, who successfully argued the case... and won."

Diamond shared more stories as they toured the rest of the house including the bath, pantry and upstairs bedrooms, and Jackson began to see the pride and strength behind the woman he'd secretly viewed as a spoiled rich girl. While walking through the home that Nicodemus had built, he felt their lust was replaced with something deeper, stronger... something that lasted longer than an orgasm's spasms, and unknowingly, the two became intoxicated with something else of which the house reeked—love. And they hadn't physically touched.

After leaving the house on the hill, Diamond made quick work of the rest of the tour, which included the hopper, presses and fermenting tanks. On the ride back, they discussed an idea that had resulted from Jackson's offhanded comment, "Y'all should do something with that house." A short time later, Diamond wheeled the cart back into the executive-offices parking lot.

"I've got it!" she said when they reached her office. "We could turn it into a standalone honeymoon suite!"

Jackson rubbed his jaw in thought. "Undergird the foundation, restore it back to its original luster with furnishings to match the era..."

"It would be so charming." Diamond reached her computer and began typing furiously, her mind abuzz. "We could even offer it as a themed wedding site, which, considering the history of this area, would go over huge!" When Jackson didn't comment, she turned and saw him reading a text with that delectable mouth set in a firm, strained line. "What is it?"

"Business," Jackson said, rising.

"Not again," Diamond responded, her voice sounding as firm as that of a military-school teacher. She stood, adding more softly, "Not like this. I care about you, Jackson, and whatever's going on with you appears more serious than a break-in. What is it?"

Jackson looked at Diamond a long moment and realized that it was the first time he'd ever heard any woman other than Aunt Evie speak to him with such raw concern. "I'm getting threats," he said evenly, his voice devoid of emotion. "Someone is vowing to kill me."

# Chapter 22

Diamond stared at Jackson a full five seconds before responding, "Kill you as in...dead?"

Jackson took a page from Genevieve Drake's book of dry wit. "What other kind of killing is there?"

"Of course, you're right. I'm just...taken aback."

Jackson walked over to a leather love seat and sat down. "It started several weeks ago, anonymous letters with no return address, and has escalated from there. Last week's break-in wasn't to steal anything. It was to leave a warning."

"What kind of warning?"

Jackson looked at Diamond, took in her genuinely disturbed expression and decided to be truthful. "Someone came in with a silencer and shot up my assistant's computer. They left a note saying the next bullet has my name on it."

"What are the police saying?"

"Nothing. We didn't go to the police."

"Why not?"

"I don't want this getting leaked to the press. My attorney hired a private investigator. He's flown into town and wants to meet with me. But his schedule is tight. He flies out tomorrow. So after a quick chat with the foreman to make sure all construction is on schedule, that's where I'm headed."

Diamond walked over to the love seat. She reached out and touched Jackson's arm. The thought of someone wanting to hurt him sent chills down her spine. She swallowed fear and summoned up courage. "You'll be fine, Jackson." She looked him dead in the eye and spoke with the confidence of God's right-hand man. "Whoever is behind this will be caught. The danger will pass."

A smile scampered across Jackson's face. "You sound pretty sure of yourself."

Diamond had to sound sure to feel sure. If something happened to Jackson, she didn't know what she'd do. "I am."

"How so? Are you going to be my protector?"

An idea instantly formed in her head. "We have people on the payroll. My father can make a call—"

Jackson spoke sternly. "No! I can handle my business." And then more softly, he said, "I gotta run, baby girl. Don't worry your pretty little head about me. Because like you said, I'll be fine."

Forty-five minutes later, Jackson sat in a living room suite at Tower 23 near downtown San Diego. Abe Swartz sat at the other end of the couch, and across from him sat one of the country's preeminent private eyes: Frank Stanton.

"I was surprised to learn that you already have news," Jackson said to the well-dressed man in the wingback chair. "You work quickly."

Frank nodded, the slightest trace of Georgian roots coming through in his accent. "Time is money. I try and spend my client's wisely."

"He's the best," Abe interjected, glad he was able to get Frank on such short notice. It hadn't hurt that he had connections with a Georgia judge who just happened to be good friends with the investigator.

"I appreciate your time." Jackson sat back and poured a glass of lemon water from the pitcher beside him. "What do you have so far?"

"For now, I'm focusing my investigation on your uncle's former colleague, Solomon Dent. He has a nephew with a criminal past. Lately, it turns out, they've been spending quite a bit of time together. This nephew, Brandon Dent, has also been spending quite a bit of time with a guy he met behind bars, a guy who just got out of prison. Now my hunch is that maybe, just maybe, some of this has to do with you."

Jackson's eyes narrowed. "Why do you think that?"

"The timing. Brandon was released from jail in August, and this cohort of his was released a few weeks ago."

When it came to Jackson's old neighborhood, more guys had gone to prison than to college. He could name a dozen people who'd experienced this fate from his block alone. "What's the dude's name?"

"Right now, all I've got is Slim Shady."

Jackson all but snorted. "That's a nickname for a rapper, Eminem."

"Okay." Frank studied Jackson a moment. "Other than the names you gave Abe, is there anyone from your past you can think of who'd want to try and hurt you?"

Jackson slowly shook his head. "I left Inglewood when I was thirteen, went back for about a month when I was sixteen and after that my focus changed." Jackson was quiet a moment, remembering how he'd gone back to the hood for his sixteenth birthday. Visiting a popular teen hangout in San Diego one day, he'd run into the cousin of one of his childhood friends. They'd talked about the neighborhood and life "back in the day." It made Jackson nostalgic to go home and reconnect. But two years away from the inner-city lifestyle had changed him. When what he'd thought was an innocent ride to the gas station turned out to be something totally different—something that ended in murder—his life forever changed. That incident spawned a determination to seek a more positive and successful path in life. "I had a long talk with my uncle, who brought me into the company as his protégé shortly after returning from this last trip to the hood," he finally continued. "I made new friends out here."

"And what about your old friends. No further contact?"

Jackson shook his head. "A lot of my old friends are either dead or in prison. But I can't think of any of them who would have a beef with me. Not one that's this deep, wanting to catch a case for murder and whatnot."

Frank reached into his inside jacket pocket and pulled out a pen and pad. "I want you to write down the names of the friends you grew up with, those guys on the block who you know went to prison."

Jackson hesitated, his street mentality kicking in. Naming names, for any reason, usually led to bad things for those involved. And then there was the note: *Your no good snitch ass.* "I don't think it's necessary, man. Like I said, I didn't have any beef with any of them."

"But one of them might have had a beef with you."

"I don't think so."

Frank shrugged. "Suit yourself. But you've obviously gotten on someone's bad side, and until we figure out who that is, I think everyone should be guilty until proven innocent. *Capiche?*"

A rash of images from Jackson's past rushed into his mind: red lights flashing while sirens blared; random, illegal car and house searches; running from police and not knowing why they chased you; being handcuffed first and asked questions later; getting pulled over for DWB: driving while Black. Yeah, he *capiche'd* all too well.

He stood. "I think you should keep the focus on Solomon Dent. I can't see anyone from the block coming for me after all these years."

Frank also stood. "Maybe not. Like I said, I'm just going on a hunch here. We'll keep Solomon in our crosshairs and a finger on his nephew, Brandon, as well. I'll be in touch."

Jackson walked over to Frank, a looming presence for a guy who was at least seven inches shorter. "You do that," he said as he shook Frank's hand. "Abe, thanks."

He left the meeting. His mind whirled. Memories he'd suppressed for decades came back full force—his past, the old life, the secrets he'd buried under the opulence of a La Jolla mansion, a booming business and the love of an uncle and aunt who'd treated him like a son. The hurt of losing them returned, along with the fear that had accompanied life in the streets with no one to guide you. Then, into the pain crept the feeling he'd experienced earlier...when he'd stared at an old brick hearth still bearing burn marks from fires long burned out. And later, he'd been struck with an assurance not felt since his parents died: *You'll be fine, Jackson. Whoever is behind this will be caught. We've got people on the payroll.* It was from his spoiled diva princess protector who'd come from generations of stock that never backed down. Jackson almost laughed out loud. A very special lady had his back. He could get used to this.

# Chapter 23

"Hi, Mom." Diamond entered the kitchen and kissed Genevieve on the cheek. Many had wondered why the wife of a wine mogul with this kind of empire would still be in the kitchen, when chefs had been hired by those with far less. The truth of the matter was that Genevieve Drake had learned the love of cooking at her mother's elbow. The act brought her joy and peace. After what she'd heard this afternoon, it was peace she needed.

"Hey, baby." Genevieve turned, then resumed stirring.

"What's for dinner? Smells delish."

"Braised short ribs served with this special pomegranate sauce."

"Yum. Grandpa's going to be happy."

"Believe it or not, he and Mama are going to a doo-wop concert at the casino. Papa Dee is a bit under the weather. It's just us tonight. Want to make the salad?"

"Mom! You know when they passed out cooking genes I was out to lunch."

"Ha! If you think making a salad is cooking, then I'd have to agree. And if it weren't for the fact that I personally taught you a few dishes, you might get away with that claim."

"I'd have to get up early to get one over on you, huh?"

"You'd better know it!"

"Okay, let me rephrase. Your daughter knows *how* to cook. She just never learned to *like* it." With that, Diamond reached for a carrot stick, dodged Genevieve's swatting spoon and left the kitchen. She reached the great room and almost ran into Dexter.

Dexter jumped back. "Slow down, fool!"

"I love you, too, brother." Diamond blew him a kiss, walked over to the wet bar and picked up an unlabeled bottle of wine. "The new pinot noir?" she questioned. "What clone is this?"

"That's old school, from the mother, baby girl. It's the real deal."

"From Papa Dee's secret arsenal?"

Dexter nodded. While all of the children had been shown the process of winemaking, Dexter was the one who'd embraced it like a second skin. He'd gotten his undergrad degree in viticulture with a minor in enology and his grad degree in business. Papa Dee's stamp of approval had come years later when after taking a sip of Dexter's creation he said, "I think this is the best wine that I've ever had." A few years later, Dexter, who also worked in business development, officially became the company's winemaker.

Diamond continued to admire the bottle. "Wow," she said, her tone almost reverent. "Can I open it?"

"Sure."

Dexter was proud of the clones he'd hoisted from vines his great-grandfather had planted more than twenty-five years ago. Using cuttings and buds from Papa Dee's original, they'd created a nice blend of fine red wines. The years 2002 and 2007 were especially good, but there was a very limited selection bottled in 1989. PNDO, Pinot Noir Drake Original, was sold for one week once a year and was available by invitation only. Those on a budget need not seek admittance to this club as the cost of one bottle equaled that of a high-end computer.

Diamond poured the wine through an aerator, filled their glasses and gave one to Dexter. There was no talking. This was serious business right here. Both of them held the glass up to the light, noting the opaqueness, the deep garnet—almost burgundy—color tinged with orange. They stuck their noses into the glass and inhaled deeply. A hint of cherry was recognized along with the blackberry fragrance. *Stellar!* After swirling their glasses for several seconds, they inhaled again. "Is that huckleberry?"

Dexter nodded. "And the slightest hint of oak."

Diamond closed her eyes and inhaled deeply. Wispy scents of cinnamon, clove and nutmeg spices ticked her nose. "The spice aromas cut through so nicely," Diamond gushed, with unabashed admiration. "But still very fruit forward. This vintage absolutely gets better with age."

Each took a quick, audible sip, letting the liquid rest on their tongues before swallowing. Dexter nodded his approval at the continued improvement of his self-proclaimed masterpiece. "Very little R.S."

Diamond nodded her agreement about residual sugar. "With just the right amount of acidity. And the low tannin level is why I prefer this to merlot."

Dexter heard voices in the foyer and looked at his watch. "Hey, sis. I need to warn you—"

"Wine tasting is over," Genevieve interrupted, sweeping

into the room with all the majesty and none of the weariness of someone who'd just whipped up a four-course meal.

Diamond hoisted her glass "It's PNDO, Mom!" she exclaimed.

"Great. Bring a couple bottles to the table. Dinner is served." She started for the door but turned to see Diamond and Dexter rooted to the spot. "Well?"

Diamond glanced at Dexter. "In a minute, Mom," he said.

"All right, son," Genevieve replied and left the room.

"What do you have to tell me?" Diamond whispered, anxiously glancing toward the hall where yet more footsteps approached. *It's just us tonight:* the statement sounded innocuous enough when her mother had said it, but now...

"Daddy knows about—"

"Diamond, Dexter," Donald interrupted, as he stepped through the entrance. As great as this space was, Donald's presence filled the room; and this had little to do with his sizable height and bulk. No, this room was filled with the authority and power afforded only to those who were not only successful and wealthy but also still in possession of common sense. "We need you now. Family meeting."

It was obvious that he wasn't leaving without them. Diamond knocked back the wine in the glass she was holding and, cutting a look at the brother she already blamed for whatever, followed her father to the room that, she had a sneaking feeling, would resemble the Inquisition before long.

# *Chapter 24*

The table was set exquisitely with Waterford crystal and bone china that had been in the family for two generations. Small talk was made as Genevieve ladled up bowls of creamy mushroom soup. Donald and Donovan dug into their servings with gusto, while Genevieve took small, ladylike sips. Dexter continued to make a meal out of the warm bread fresh from the oven, slathered with butter and homemade jam, while Diamond felt small drops of soup collide with the knot in her stomach.

Finally, she'd had enough of the tension. She placed her napkin on her lap and spoke to the room at large. "Out with it already, jeez! What is going on?"

Genevieve looked at Donald.

Donovan looked at Genevieve.

Diamond glanced at Dexter, who'd suddenly become transfixed by something at the bottom of his wineglass.

Donald eyed the jewel of the family, his only daughter,

whom he'd protect with his life. He finished his bite and put down his napkin. "I received some disturbing news today, honey. About Jackson Wright."

Diamond turned to Dexter. If looks could kill, she'd be up on murder charges right about now.

"We know you're seeing him, and no, Dexter did not tell us."

"Who did?" Belatedly, Diamond realized that this hastily blurted question may not have been the proper rebuttal. How many times had this *Law & Order* fan heard the buzz word: deny, deny, *deny!*

"He heard it through the grapevine, literally," Donovan said, with an unceremonious scraping of his silver spoon against the now empty soup bowl.

"After Roberto saw y'all *in* the grapevine," Genevieve clarified.

*Where had the head grower been hiding?* And aside from the fact that she'd enjoyed his kisses…hadn't she told Jackson to behave? This was all his fault! "What is with the interrogation?" she asked saucily, figuring that the best offense might be a good defense. "I was over twenty-one, last time I checked."

"And the last time *I* checked, your workday started around nine and ended around six," Donald easily countered. "When I suggested you give Jackson a tour, necking in the fields isn't what I had in mind."

"Now, Donald," Genevieve intervened, memories of parts of the land she and Donald had christened rising up as fresh as the bread that sat on the table. "Let's keep the focus on what's important here."

Diamond crossed her arms. "And what's that?"

The way Donald took his time and placed a healthy rib on his plate, you'd think what was important was his dinner. The conversation lulled as everyone but Diamond helped themselves to braised ribs and warm potato salad. After taking a bite, he continued, "I had Jackson checked out."

"Dad, you background everyone who does business with us. And?"

"And when I hired his construction company for our renovation, our check was limited primarily to his business background. After I discovered your interest in him, I determined that a little more digging was in order."

"And I'm determining that you need to mind your own business." Donald shot Diamond a stern look. "Sorry, Dad. I don't mean to be disrespectful. I'm just…frustrated that you felt the need for a full-out investigation."

Diamond was angry but not overly surprised. Theirs was a close-knit family, who knew the goings-on in each other's lives. As the only daughter, Diamond's personal life seemed especially prone to the microscopic interest of both her parents and brothers, and seeing her walk down the aisle was one of Genevieve's utmost desires—one that had intensified after Diamond turned twenty-nine.

"Daughter—" Donald waited until Diamond looked at him "—in the words of Richard Nixon, let me make one thing perfectly clear." Donald methodically wiped barbeque sauce off his fingers. "I don't care if you live to be a hundred and marry five times…you are first and foremost a Drake, whose safety and welfare will always be my business." Diamond stared at her father, waiting for him to continue. "Now, normally I wouldn't have found this out so quickly, but it just so happens that a guy in the L.A. Sheriff's office was a classmate of mine."

"Lucky you."

Knowing she was upset, Donald gave his daughter a pass. "That luck as you call it continued, because when I mentioned his name it turns out that his sister knows Jackson Wright's mother."

"You sure you don't want to take your chances in Vegas?" Diamond mumbled. "'Cause you're on a roll."

"That's enough, Diamond." Genevieve's voice was soft yet firm—that iron-fist-in-velvet-glove trick that she'd perfected.

"Jackson Wright was born Jackson Burnett. He grew up in the streets of L.A., and while no criminal record was found, word has it that he dabbled in gang activity. His mother, Sharon Burnett, became strung out on drugs, eventually driving under the influence and committing vehicular manslaughter. The victims were a mother and her two children. She received twenty-five to life and is currently incarcerated at a prison in central California."

No one ate. Movement was slight. Donald continued.

"When Jackson was thirteen, he went to live with his uncle, John Wright, Sharon's half brother. John adopted him, took him under his wing and produced the man we see today. I believe he's a good man, Diamond, but I also believe you have a right to know what he once was."

Diamond looked at her father. "The past is the past, Dad. If you think he's a good man, then why tell me all of this?"

"Has Jackson told you?" The look on Diamond's face told everyone that he had not.

"You need to know the type of man you're dealing with, Diamond," Genevieve said softly, her eyes full of compassion. "Someone who has been abandoned, betrayed and lived through some very tough situations. There may be emotional scars there that make commitment difficult. Honey, we've seen the hurt that Benjamin caused and want you to be very clear as you move forward before you become more involved. That's all."

"Don't sweat it, big sis," Dexter said, to lighten the mood. When it came to serious, heavy scenes…he'd rather not, thank you very much. "You know my frat conference is coming up soon. Some big ballers will be there for sure. I'll keep an eye out."

"Myles keeps asking about you," Donovan offered, referring to one of his golfing buddies.

"Myles has children my age," Diamond shot back.

Donovan laughed. "Not quite. He's forty-eight and in great shape. Besides, his two twenty-something children live with their mother in Phoenix."

Diamond placed her napkin on the table. "I'm not interested." She stood. "Please excuse me."

Diamond reached her living quarters in the east wing and paced the length of it. Thoughts from the dinner conversation crowded her mind like the Times Square crowd on New Year's Eve. What her father had shared was bad enough but worse was how this information was potentially connected to what Jackson had told her this afternoon: that someone was trying to kill him.

Faster and faster the thoughts came. *Jackson. Adopted. Commitment issues. Born Jackson Burnett. Mom in prison. Gang activity. Abandoned. Betrayed. Emotional scars. Adopted. Not Jackson Wright, Jackson Burnett. Betrayed. Abandoned. Prison. Difficult. Commitment. Difficult. Commitment. Difficult. Somebody's trying to kill me!* Diamond's hands went to her ears.

Beep. Beep. The call tone was a welcomed intrusion on her thoughts. She snatched up the phone, looked at the caller ID and her heart dropped. Having no idea how the conversation would play out, she answered, "Hello, Jackson."

"Hey, baby." His voice was low, sexy and oozing with desire.

"Hello, Jackson." Diamond closed her eyes, all too aware that she sounded like the proverbial broken record and that her voice held all the warmth of an ice cube.

"You said that already." Pause. "What's wrong?"

Diamond gripped her iPhone and again paced the room. "Just left a family meeting. There's a lot going on."

"Care to share?"

*Do you care to share?* A beat and then, "I'd rather talk about you. How did the meeting with the investigator go?"

"It went all right. He had a few leads. They're working on it."

"What about you? Have you thought more about who could be behind the notes, break-in and gunshots?"

"Not really. That's what I'm paying Frank to do."

"Frank?"

"Yeah, the private eye."

"Have you ever considered, I mean, I don't know much about your background—" *only, like, everything* "—but do you think it could be someone from your past, your childhood?" Silence. Not good. She knew she was treading on dangerous ground, but she needed to know that Jackson trusted her and that he would confide in her. She wanted him to tell her what she now knew. "Jackson? Did you hear me?"

"I heard you."

There was an even longer hesitation and then this: "What difference does it make? You're still going to have my back, right, no matter who it is?"

"Of course."

"All right, then."

"Tell me about your childhood, Jackson."

"Why?" Diamond knew he was angry, could imagine him standing, pacing. "What does my childhood have to do with you?"

"You have to do with me, baby. Where you come from is a part of that. It helps me know you better, the way you knew me better once I told you about Papa Dee and Nicodemus."

"Yeah, well, my history ain't nothing like that."

"I'd still like to know it."

"No. You wouldn't. Look, I don't want to talk about this anymore."

"Well, I do!" *Okay, playing the demanding princess card is probably not the best tactic.* Diamond softened her voice. "Baby, do you think it matters to me where you come from or how you grew up?"

"Looks like it. You're questioning me like you're Johnny Cochran. I'm halfway expecting you to bring out a glove."

"I just want to know, that's all. Maybe this is a conversation best had in person. Can I come over?"

There was a pause long enough you could drive a train through it and then, "Hell, no."

Click.

"I know this man did not just hang up on me." Diamond stared at the phone as if it had the answer. She couldn't snatch up her purse fast enough, and even though she knew that it was irrational—that hot nights and sticky thighs had not only blurred the professional boundary but obliterated it and, with it, her employer clout—she reverted back to the familiar: being the boss. And a man who reported to her, okay...kinda, sorta...had overstepped his bounds. Before the night was over, she determined, he would know that that was sooo not okay.

# *Chapter 25*

Jackson sat in the darkness—brooding. The only thing rarer than the vintage cognac he nursed from a tumbler was the fact that the drink was in his hand. He was an occasional one-glass wino, a "have a beer with the fellas" kind of man— one more keen to have a six-pack on his body than one in the fridge. Sure, he'd smoked a little weed in his day, much like others in the neighborhood where he grew up, but for the most part, Jackson liked to have his wits about him. But he'd been searching for those wits ever since getting off the phone with Diamond. *Tell me about your childhood, Jackson.* This curiosity with his roots had seemingly come out of nowhere. Her request, the break-in and Frank's questioning about friends from his past had forced his mind back to a time he'd felt best left forgotten: his other life, his mother. He thought of their last meeting, and tears welled up in his eyes. *No!* Jackson had spent too much time lamenting things he couldn't change. Determined to stay focused on the future and not the past, he tossed back the drink, snatched up his keys and bounded from the house. The names of several women crossed his mind: any one of which could help him push back those things he'd rather not think about. Bypassing the Maserati, he jumped into his least expensive but most treasured vehicle: the Jeep his aunt and uncle had bought him. He whizzed down the drive, opened the gate…and came headlight to headlight with Diamond Drake.

It was lights, camera, action all right, but this drama was all too real. Jackson jumped out of his Jeep and strode to the driver's side of Diamond's BMW. "What are you doing here?"

It was not quite the welcome she expected, but since she'd had time to do some thinking on the drive over, it was one that she understood. "I need to talk to you."

"What about? My *childhood?*"

"About a lot of things."

"Well, you should have called first. As you can see, I'm on my way out."

"This shouldn't take long, Jackson. I've come all this way."

"Then you'll know how to get back to where you came from, won't you? Move your car." Jackson turned and headed back to his vehicle.

Diamond jumped out of hers. "I'm not going anywhere!"

Jackson stopped and spun around.

"You heard me," Diamond hissed, arms crossed, legs spread, balancing herself on three-inch spikes as if doing so on cobblestone was an everyday occurrence. "I'm not leaving until we talk."

The look on Jackson's face as he approached her caused Diamond's breath to catch in her throat. While his expression was unreadable, his eyes flashed with intense anger, and his body was taut with restraint. Diamond wanted to gobble him up and run for cover at the same time.

He walked up to her, almost nipple to nipple, so close that their breaths mingled. "What did you say?"

In light of his skulking presence it was difficult, but the little girl who'd held her own with two rambunctious brothers held her ground here. She channeled Nicodemus and Papa Dee.

Several tense seconds passed between them.

"All right, princess." Jackson slowly backed away from her. "Enter at your own risk."

Diamond watched Jackson get into his car. He backed up and waited. So did she. Suddenly, she didn't feel so confident. *Enter at your own risk? What does that mean?* Her mother's words sounded in her left ear: *You need to know the type of man you're dealing with...* Genevieve was right. She really didn't know Jackson—clarification: she knew Jackson *Wright,* not Jackson *Burnett.* Her father's words filtered through her right ear: *I believe that Jackson is a good man.* Decision made, Diamond walked to her car and soon followed Jackson into his estate. Through her rearview mirror, she watched the gates close behind her. Her heart pounded. But she was inside and the gates were closed. There was no turning back.

Once parked, Jackson took a couple steps, then turned and looked at her. "Well?" When she said nothing, he shook his head and walked inside. She followed him. He walked into a well-appointed living room: warm earth tones with splashes of red, the understated elegance of a designer's touch. He walked over to a chair and sat. There were no offers for her to do so, no invitations to water, wine or a turn in the turret.

*What the hell am I doing here?*

Outside the gates, she'd been too filled with the items on her own agenda to pay much attention to his appearance. But now she took in the black button-down shirt that was tucked into equally black slacks. His copper-toned skin looked creamy smooth against the fabric, and she could tell that the understated platinum jewelry he wore had not been purchased at a discount store. She looked into his eyes, and along with anger and impatience, she saw something else—sadness. In her mind, she could imagine the little boy with a druggie mother, no father and seemingly no way out of a bad situation. Her feelings were as jumbled as uncooked ramen noodles, but in this moment, she decided to speak simply, directly and from the heart.

"Earlier I asked about your childhood, but the fact of the matter is...I already know."

Jackson crossed his arms. "Know what?"

"About...your past." She looked at him, and in that moment if given a choice would rather have stared down a Category 5 hurricane. "It's standard procedure for our company to check out anyone connected to the vineyard." She hadn't asked but felt sure God would forgive her this small white lie.

"I'm not connected to Drake Wines."

"But you're intimately involved with a major expansion, for millions of dollars."

Once adopted, Jackson's uncle had gone to great lengths to "protect" him. Files had been purchased, records erased. His eyes narrowed. "Just what is it that you think you know?"

Diamond knew that if there was ever any chance of gaining his trust she had to tell him the truth. "I know that you were born Jackson Burnett, were adopted by your uncle and that your mother is in prison."

His reaction was immediate—and explosive. "My past is none of your damn business," he said, shooting out of the chair. "And that ain't some background-check information. You had to know somebody, pay money for that!"

Diamond took a step toward him. "My dad found out we were...involved—"

"Oh, and let me guess—he made a phone call. Like the

one you were going to make for me earlier? When I trusted you and told you what was going on at my company? How long have you known this, huh? Since you met me? Was that the appeal? Thought you'd come down from your castle and hang out with somebody who used to live in the hood? Am I the closest you could get to a gangster?" Even though he'd been cleared of any involvement, Jackson always felt ashamed about what had happened at the gas station. Call it guilt by association, but Jackson felt as responsible as those behind bars for what had gone down.

"Jackson, that's not fair."

"And what you did is?" Jackson wondered just how much Diamond's father had been able to uncover and whether his money had been as effective as Uncle John's. "You know I was adopted. You know my mom is in prison. What else do you know?"

*My God, is there more?* "That's it. My father received this news today and told me tonight, right before I called you."

"And instead of telling me what you knew straight out, you decided to play games. *Tell me about your childhood, Jackson,*" he mimicked. "This is ridiculous."

"Okay, maybe you're right. Maybe that wasn't the best approach. I was in shock. I was confused. But I'm here. Doesn't that say something?" Silence. "He only did it because he knows that I have feelings for you. *Deep* feelings, Jackson. Some would call him overprotective—"

"Overprotective, hell. He's stepped way out-of-bounds, Diamond. And so have you!"

"It's only because he loves me so much." Diamond saw the flash of hurt in Jackson's eyes and realized how her words may have made him feel. He'd had an aunt who'd adored him and an uncle who'd raised him with love and respect, but he didn't know his biological father...had never felt his love. She took a step toward him. "I'm sorry for what happened to you, Jackson."

"Uh-huh, cool. Get out."

She took another step. "I don't care about your past. I believe that you're a good man."

"You had no right to delve into my background. If I'd wanted you to know about it, I would have told you."

Realization dawned. *He's ashamed. Even though the circumstances weren't his fault, he's ashamed about not knowing his father and about what his mother did.* "It was an intrusion, and for that, I'm sorry. But I don't apologize for caring about you."

"I mean it, Diamond. I want you to leave." Jackson's entire body was tense.

But where Jackson felt anger, Diamond saw only fear. She took another step. "I don't apologize for loving you."

His chest rose and fell with the intensity of his breathing as he fought to keep the pain from the past at bay and maintain control of his emotions.

Diamond took one last step and came face-to-face with her heartbeat. She tentatively reached up and caressed his face. A single tear slid down her cheek. "I love you, Jackson Wright."

One second passed...two...five. He grabbed her, crushed her to his chest. She could feel the rapidity of his heartbeat. She put her arms around him, wishing she could love his hurt away. She knew that might not be possible, but at the very least, she could ease it for awhile.

"You said to enter at my own risk, right?"

"Yes," Jackson mumbled, barely above a whisper.

"Well, mister, you're the one who's in trouble."

"How?"

"Because I want to assault your body. I want to feel you

inside me, long and deep." She stepped back, looked into his eyes. "Will you make love to me, Jackson?"

His eyes immediately darkened with desire. In answer, he swept her up and headed for the stairs.

# Chapter 26

Jackson reached the double staircase, but instead of taking the one that led to his master suite, he went in the other direction. After setting Diamond down as if she were a fragile treasure, he took her hand and walked down a short hall with a door at the end. He opened it, revealing yet another stairway. Wordlessly, they mounted the steps, and when Jackson opened the door at the top of the climb, Diamond's eyes widened. They were outside, in the turret she'd seen earlier, with a 360-degree view of San Diego County. Her eyes took in the magnificence of the night: twinkling city lights in one direction, the ocean before them and stars above. Jackson's eyes were for her alone.

He reached for her and placed a kiss on her forehead. It was soft, almost reverent, and Diamond teared up at its sincerity. He kissed one temple and then the other, all the while reaching for the zipper on the front of her dress and pulling it down…farther and farther…exposing her warm skin to the cool of the night. Her nipples pebbled as the wind caressed them—barely concealed in a sheer mesh bra—and as Jackson's mouth found hers, he forced his tongue inside.

He kissed her, tenderly, fervently, whirling his tongue inside her mouth as his finger swirled around her nipple. Diamond shuddered as his hands roamed her upper body, and he buried his hand in her hair, pulling her even closer and deepening the exchange. The assault was so intense that Diamond's knees almost buckled. But there was no need to worry. Jackson was ahead of her, and even now, he was leading her to a low-sitting platform covered with colorful pillows of various sizes and textures that occupied one wall of the circular outdoor room. She eased down on the pillows, and after hurriedly taking off his clothes, he joined her there, massaging her skin, licking her nipples through the soft mesh, fingering her paradise, driving her wild. Diamond gasped as his tongue trailed down her body, lingering at her stomach and navel before he went down farther and kissed her thighs.

"You're so soft," he whispered, kissing the insides of her thighs and then blowing on the wetness. Closer and closer he came to her heat, only to place a trail of kisses back down her legs all the way to her toes, where he sucked them one by one. Diamond was out of her mind with desire. Her body thrashed with impatience and the knowledge of what was to come.

Jackson wouldn't be hurried. He kissed a path back up her legs, hips, stomach and breasts and seared her with another hot, wet kiss.

"Jackson, please."

He chuckled and made his way back down, spreading her wide and parting her folds with his sharp, talented tongue. Over and again he licked her, flicking her nub while placing a finger inside, heightening her pleasure, taking her over the edge. At the height of her orgasm, and with no thoughts of condoms by either of them, he slowly eased himself inside of her, her heat pulsating around inch after delicious inch. He filled her to the core, pulled out and then filled her again. Over and over, deeper and deeper, slowly, oh…so…slowly he loved her, twisting his hips from side to side, setting up a rhythm that would be known to them alone. She grabbed his ass and pulled him closer still, her legs in the air as she spread them to accommodate his expanding girth, tears of ecstasy now on a free flow. He got up and pulled her with him, walked them over to a part of the turret that jutted out over his well-landscaped yard. The infinity pool glistened against the darkened sky; the lights of San Diego continued to beckon in the distance.

But Diamond couldn't see; she could only feel as Jackson came up behind her, held her hips and entered her again. That they were naked and standing outside added to the friction and her delight. He kneaded her backside, running his hands over her flesh as he pounded her over and again. The wind blew, and goose bumps broke out on Diamond's flesh. It began to rain, but their dance continued. There was something about making love outside that felt naughty and decadent, even as it felt organic and pure. He lifted her onto him, placed her back to the wall and entered her again. The intensity of his thrusts intensified, his tongue mimicking his hip movements as he kissed her senseless. He pounded her relentlessly, as if he could go on forever. She wished he would. The rain outside, her lover inside her, Diamond felt herself explode again. This time, Jackson joined her. They both saw stars, and neither was looking at the sky.

## Chapter 27

"Come on, baby." Jackson wrapped Diamond in a throw he retrieved from a chest. They went inside and were soon enjoying the warm water pulsating from the multiple jets in Jackson's master bath. Diamond admired his body as she rubbed a fresh, lemony-scented soap all over it, kneading the tension from his neck and shoulder muscles much as he'd done to her not long ago. They rubbed their soapy bodies against each other, bringing themselves once again to arousal. Neither could get enough. With all of the lovemaking that had occurred one might not have thought it possible, but when Diamond's hand went around his limp shaft, it immediately sprang to life and along with it, Diamond's desire. She wanted to satisfy Jackson as much as he'd satisfied her and soon found herself kissing him all over. Her tongue was akin to molten lava, scorching his shoulders and broad expanse of chest. She tongued his navel and discovered a secret. He was ticklish. Then she dipped her head lower and his laughter turned into a satisfied moan. She wrapped her mouth around him, licking him like a lollipop with a prize inside. Again water served as the backdrop as these two lovers explored and enjoyed each other. Diamond loved Jackson so tenderly, so completely that it was almost his undoing. He grabbed the hand that rested at his waist, pulled her up and took the lead. Wordlessly, he walked them over to the bench on the shower's far wall. He sat down and so did Diamond—on him. And just like that, once again, he was in her—filling her full, loving her deeply, leaving no room for anything else, especially doubt. Diamond leaned forward. Blood rushed to her head the way love was rushing to her heart. She was overcome with passion and emotion, marveling at the fact that there was this much ardency in the world. He reached around for her nipples, grabbing and squeezing as she continued to jump for joy on his joystick, increasing the pace and their pleasure with each rise and rotation. If their cries had been a song, it would have been in perfect harmony. Her high-pitched whimpers matched his low, deep grunts. Their worlds exploded. When it was over, they sat gasping for breath, grasping for an explanation to this insatiable hunger.

"Baby," Jackson said when his breathing returned to normal, "it's time to shower again."

A short time later, they lay in Jackson's custom-made bed. Diamond's sated body spooned against his; a high-thread-count sheet rested over their bodies. She knew she could stay here forever, in his arms. His parentage didn't matter. His past was of no consequence. Her heart just might get broken again, but she wasn't going anywhere far from this man—not if she could help it. Theirs was a companionable silence. Diamond thought Jackson had fallen asleep, but he hadn't.

"My first memory is when I was three or four years old," he said, his voice soft, his breath hot and wet against her earlobe. "A fair came to the neighborhood. You know, one of those traveling kinds where they set up a Ferris wheel, Tilt-A-Whirl, Spider and whatnot? They set up in a grocery store parking lot right down the street from where we lived. I don't remember what I rode, probably a merry-go-round at that age, but I remember all the lights and the people. Oh, and the cotton candy. It's crazy how your mind recalls things, but I remember pulling that confection off the stick and stuffing it into my mouth. It was blue, and I thought the way it disappeared in my mouth was magic. I must have eaten three or four of those things.

"My next really strong memory is a few years later, when I was around seven. I came home from school and noticed that Mom was acting strange. She was talking fast, and her eyes were glazed. She was high, of course, but my young mind didn't grasp that right away. She left, came back with a hamburger and fries and told me to watch TV until she got back. I didn't see her for a week."

Diamond turned to face Jackson, who was now lying on his back, staring at the ceiling. She couldn't believe what she was hearing. *What kind of mother would leave her child like that?* She placed a hand on his chest and whispered, "You must have been so scared."

"The first day I wasn't. Thought it was kind of nice to stay up late, watching TV, eating almost a whole box of Cap'n Crunch. But the next day, when I came home from school and she still wasn't there…that's when I began to worry."

"She was out getting high?"

Jackson nodded. "And doing whatever it took to support her habit. The day after she came back, I came home from school to a houseful of people—my mom's boyfriend at the time and some of his friends. He was from New York and had brought back this new drug, one sweeping across the five boroughs faster than a plane streaks across the sky—crack cocaine. Alvin Johnson. That was the name of the man who ruined my mother's life and mine in the process. I hate him to this day."

To this point, Diamond had considered hate a draining, nonproductive emotion. But in this instance, it was the only one that made sense. "That's who your mom was picking up when she had the accident?"

"Yes, but that was years later, when I was thirteen. By then, I was pretty hard myself, had taken to petty crimes and being the lookout for a fairly high-ranking drug dealer. I was just getting ready to move into the big leagues—dealing— when she got arrested. That's when my uncle stepped in and saved my life."

"Had you known him before?"

"Vaguely. I remember him coming around a few times, him and my mom arguing. He told her to go into treatment, and she told him to go to hell." Jackson laughed, but his voice held no humor. "I was only in the system two days before he came and got me. I don't know what he did or said to her, but my mom terminated her rights almost immediately after-ward. John and Evie Wright adopted me the following year, and became the parents I'd never had. That's when my life changed for the better. I've not looked back." Jackson shifted uncomfortably, turned to look at Diamond.

She looked back, eyes filled with love...and nonjudgment. He continued staring at her, and she would have sworn that a tear was forming in his eye when he looked away. "Jackson... what is it?" Her voice was soft, quizzical.

Again, she wondered if he would say anything. But finally he did. "I went back one time."

Diamond said nothing, just turned, laid her head on his chest and lazily ran her hand up and down his arm.

"The end of July, the weekend of my sixteenth birthday, I ran into the cousin of a dude I grew up with. It felt good seeing somebody from the old neighborhood. Until that point, I didn't even realize that I'd missed them. I told him that it was my birthday, and he said I should celebrate with the boys. I told him it sounded like a plan.

"My birthday was on a Friday that year. I told Uncle John and Aunt Evie I wanted to celebrate in my old neighborhood. They weren't crazy about the idea but finally gave their consent to my leaving. I hit the block, and it was like I never left. I meant to stay three days and stayed almost a month— partying, drinking, getting high, having fun. My boys almost had me convinced that I needed to move back there, that I could stay with one of them. I asked about school, but they waved that comment away. 'We're making more paper than the teachers,' they told me. And it was true."

"How were they doing that?"

"Selling drugs. And other illegal activities."

Diamond paused, her mind filled with what "illegal activities" could entail. "What made you come back home—to La Jolla?"

"I got a wake-up call."

Jackson became silent then. Diamond thought he'd gone to sleep, but when she looked at him she saw that his eyes were gazing at the ceiling. She wondered about the wake-up call, but clearly it was something he did not want to talk about. "When was the last time you saw your mom?"

Jackson was silent for another long moment. He swallowed once, again tamping down a dam of emotions that threatened to spill over into the bed and this new life. "About five years ago." His voice was low, reflective, laced with heaviness. "Went to see her at the prison. Asked her about my father, my biological. She told me it was Alvin. I called her a liar. It was an ugly scene. She cursed me out, told me never to come back there. All these years later and she's still choosing him over me. I vowed to never see her again."

"But Jackson," she said, her heart aching with the pain of these revelations. "She's your mother."

"Evie Wright was my mother," Jackson hissed. "And she's dead. And as far as I'm concerned, Sharon Burnett is dead, too. I've cut her out of my life."

"But what about your heart?"

"There, too." That's what he said. But the lone, almost imperceptible tear that fell from his eye suggested otherwise.

"I'm sorry about what happened to you, baby. Those experiences would have crushed a lesser man."

"Yeah, well, they almost did me in."

"But they didn't. You survived and thrived, and for that I'm so grateful. I love you, Jackson."

Five seconds passed. Ten. Fifteen.

Jackson's arms tightened around her. "I love you, too."

# Chapter 28

Jackson and Diamond talked into the night. Dawn was streaking across the sky when she left his mansion, her heart full of love and dreams of a life with him. And more than what she'd ever hoped for had happened. He'd told her he loved her! This single declaration energized her, replaced the sleep she'd exchanged for a night of lovemaking. When she entered the great room for the meeting that had been arranged before the Wright/Burnett revelation, she was awake, aware and ready for action.

"Good morning, everybody," she fairly sang into the room.

Genevieve's brow rose oh-so-slightly. "Sounds like you've had a very good morning."

"Morning, sis," Dexter mumbled around a freshly baked croissant, sent to the main house by David and Mary's chef.

Various greetings continued along with small talk as Donovan and Grandpa David entered the room. Papa Dee was the last to arrive, his steps precise and unhurried. He sat, accepted a cup of coffee and waited for the meeting to begin.

Diamond took a last sip of her green tea and began, her tone as businesslike as her tailored navy suit. "Has everyone reviewed the proposal I emailed yesterday?"

Nods and affirmatives resounded.

"As I stated in the outline, I believe that restoring Papa Dee's house to its original luster, while updating it with a pristine, top-of-the-line kitchen and spa bath, will create the buzz to make this a destination wedding location—especially after we install the Jacuzzi behind it and build a gazebo at the crest of the hill, for actual weddings, anniversaries and other such ceremonies to take place."

"Nice work, daughter," Donald said, pride evident in his voice. "We've been wondering what to do with Grandpa's house for some time. I think this is a brilliant idea."

"It's all right," Dexter drawled, all too ready to lessen the chance of any serious head swelling. "But if we're going to have all different types of ceremonies there, we can't call it a honeymoon suite."

Diamond typed away on her iPad.

"This is good stuff," Donovan chimed in. "But I think we should limit gatherings to those on the smaller scale, say a hundred guests or less. That way, we can focus on the quality and take into account parking, accommodations, et cetera."

"But the suite would be available to whomever, correct?" Genevieve asked. "Not just to those who get married on our property."

"Yes," Diamond answered. "The suite would be booked on a first come, first serve basis."

"I especially like the idea of a chef and butler attending to the honeymooners or whomever stays there," Genevieve continued. "Perhaps Mom Mary will even do the honors of preparing a signature dessert, based on one of Papa Dee's favorites."

"Well, that would be pralines, hands down," Papa Dee said, his voice raspy, eyes bright. "My mama used to make batches of 'em every Christmas and hand them out to the folk in the neighborhood."

"We could include them in the welcome basket along with a couple bottles of our sparkling wines, gourmet cheese, nuts, crackers, fruits." Diamond typed these suggestions as well, her excitement growing with every keystroke. "Perhaps I'll do a simple brochure detailing the history of the house and include a picture of Papa."

"You're getting ready to be famous, old man," Dexter teased, leaning over to pat Papa Dee on the back. "People coming from all over just to see your birthplace."

"Aw, you go on now," Papa replied. But his eyes twinkled.

Ever the businessman, Donald shifted gears from nostalgia to numbers. "What's the cost of this addition?"

"That ground will be covered in the meeting I've scheduled for this afternoon, where Jackson and Taylor will be in attendance." She made sure to sound as businesslike as possible, but at the mention of his name a soft flush crept from her neck to her hairline. "I know it's short notice, but hopefully we can all make it. I want the restored home to be unveiled along with the rest of Drake Wines Resort & Spa, and I definitely want it included in the *O Magazine* shoot happening in late January."

Genevieve watched as her daughter tried to maintain a businesslike veneer. But she'd seen the flush and knew the look. She'd *worn* that look many times after Donald had thoroughly and completely satisfied her. "Sweetheart, how did you come up with this wonderful idea?"

Diamond took a calming breath and answered, "It was inspired by a comment Jackson made as we were touring the grounds. He was quite impressed with the quality of work-manship and thought, as we do, that it should not only be preserved but enjoyed."

"Is the house all he's enjoying?" Donald asked.

"No, Dad. It isn't. You'll all bug me until I tell you anyway, so I'll say it outright. Jackson and I are officially dating. And I'm officially in love with him."

Donald and Genevieve exchanged glances. Donovan sat back in his chair and sighed. Dexter chuckled.

"I know what you all might be thinking about Jackson's past. But I'm not dating the boy who left Inglewood when he was thirteen. I'm dating a caring, thoughtful, amazing man who now runs a multimillion-dollar company. This is my life and my decision. When it comes to me and Jackson, please respect my wishes…and back off."

Later, the family met again. This time, it was in the conference room in the center of the building that housed the Drake Vineyard executive offices. David, Mary, Donald, Genevieve, Donovan, Dexter and Diamond had been joined by Jackson and Taylor. For ninety-eight-year-old Papa Dee, it was nap time. He was not present. Normally the elder Drakes would not be present either, but since this was a family heirloom of sorts, Diamond wanted their contributions. The meeting went smoothly, and after a drive out to the house on the hill, and a walk-through with all parties coming together on the plans for Papa Dee's birthplace—whose official name would become the Papa Dee Suite—the plans were approved.

"I'm very excited about these plans," Taylor said as she, Diamond and Jackson headed to the cart that Diamond had driven. "I already have some ideas that I believe would be perfect to both capture the turn-of-the-century feel when this home was built and give it the luxuriousness that a honeymoon haven and the like demands."

Diamond smiled at Taylor. "I can't wait. How soon can we meet?"

"The rest of my week is jam-packed, and my parents' anniversary party is this weekend, but I can get my staff started on creating three proposed looks. I can also have them gather fabric swatches, search for furniture… Would Tuesday or Wednesday of next week work?"

"How long have your parents been married?"

"Thirty years," Taylor proudly answered.

"I'm so glad the accident with your father wasn't more serious."

"He's zipping around on the golf course as if it never happened."

"That's wonderful, Taylor. It's important that we take time out and celebrate what's really important. Tuesday or Wednesday sounds fine to me," Diamond continued, back to business. "But that only gives us two weeks for construction. Jackson, how do you feel about that?"

Jackson shrugged. "It's doable. But we're going to have to get cranking and work around the clock. I'll also have to subcontract some of the work with a couple other construction companies. They're quite reputable and ones I've often worked with, so this won't be a problem. With the expanded plans we've already added to the hotel's dining and lounge areas, and now this… Let me speak to my foreman and let you know by end of business day today."

He was just getting ready to jump into the back of Diamond's cart when Donald drove up in his. "Boss, why don't you come along with me? I want to run a couple things past you."

"Sure, Donald." He gave Diamond's shoulder a quick squeeze and then walked past the cart that carried Donovan and Dexter to the one where Donald sat waiting. He hopped in and Donald began the hundred-plus-yard trek from the house on the hill to the office. "I have to tell you, sir…it's a wonderful opportunity for me to restore that house up there. With all of the history it holds and what it means to your family, not to mention those who'll begin their lives together under its roof, well, it's an honor."

"We feel really good about it—especially my grandfather. He'll be thrilled about the slab you've suggested, honoring our forefather, Nicodemus. And speaking of honor—" Donald continued, reaching the executive offices and shutting off the engine while turning to look Jackson in the eye "—I'd like to know your intentions where my daughter is concerned."

## Chapter 29

The air fairly crackled between these two strong, powerful men as Donald awaited his answer. Just then, Donovan and Dexter pulled up beside them and exited their cart. They saw Donald and Jackson eyeing each other and paused. The look told the brothers that they'd been on one accord: that Donald was now asking Jackson the question they'd pondered on their way down. They walked to Jackson's cart without hesitation. Three pairs of chocolate-brown Drake eyes stared at Jackson, who looked up and saw Diamond and Taylor approaching. "Let's take this powwow into your office," he suggested to Donald, jumping out of the cart as he did so. "And then I can share exactly what is on my mind."

The men entered Donald's office. He closed the door. The four men painted a formidable picture: all tall, dark, handsome, exuding testosterone and confidence to the nth power. Jackson looked just as capable of kicking butt and taking names as a Drake on any day. His air of authority gave one the indication that he believed this about himself, as well.

"I care about your daughter," he said to Donald. "Your sister," he said to Donovan and Dexter. "I have no intention of hurting her." The Drake men relaxed their shoulders somewhat, but their stances remained firm. "I respect the Drake name but am not intimidated by it, which is why I want to make myself clear on any issue regarding myself, my company and/or my family. If you want to know something…ask me." He looked at Donald. "With all due respect, sir, your conducting an investigation into my life was way out of line."

"When it comes to my daughter, there are no rules of conduct," Donald replied. "I'd do it again in a heartbeat."

"We're a close-knit family who protects our own and have each other's backs at all times." Dexter took a step in Jackson's direction. "Do you have a problem with that?"

"No problem," Jackson casually answered. "As long as it doesn't happen again."

"As long as Diamond is happy, we're cool," Donovan countered. "Don't start none, won't be none."

The merest smile scampered across Jackson's face. "That's probably something you should discuss with Diamond. But my guess is…she's very satisfied. Now, gentlemen, if you'll excuse me I have a five-star hotel to finish building and a homestead to renovate." He reached out and shook each man's hand, then walked out of the office with back straight and head held high.

The men watched him leave. "What do you think?" Donald asked, after a moment.

"Good man," Donovan answered.

"No doubt," Dexter agreed.

"We could do worse than a successful construction company owner in the family," Donald said.

"Absolutely." Dexter rubbed his chin thoughtfully. "In fact, it might be time for me to build my dream home. Get the family discount, you feel me?"

The men laughed. "Let's just hope his dating Diamond has a better ending than she and Benjamin did," Donovan said, concern for his sister showing in his eyes.

"Yes, let's hope," Donald agreed. "Because if he hurts my daughter, he'll answer to me. And I mean that."

Down the hall, Diamond paced. She called Kathleen. "Are they out yet? Have you seen anyone?"

"No, dear, and I've been looking." Kathleen hadn't felt this type of drama since *As The World Turns* had left the air. "I'll buzz you as soon as I know."

"Okay." Diamond remained tense. She'd seen the men talking when she drove up with Taylor and watched them walk into the building. Had Taylor not wanted to get clear on a few decor points, she would have marched down the hall and into the room right behind them. As it was, she was beside herself with curiosity. Her dad and brothers were a formidable bunch. But then...so was Jackson.

Diamond's cell phone rang. "Hi, Mom."

"Hello, darling. Do you have a moment?"

"Yes."

"Good. Can you come by the house? I'd like to have a little chat."

Diamond was torn. She wanted to talk to her mom but equally wanted to stand by should a referee be needed. The desire to confide in Genevieve won out. She trusted Jackson to hold his own.

"Kat, I'm going to see Mom for a moment."

"You're not going to wait—"

"Until the dust settles? Not now. But if you hear a rumble, give me a call."

Genevieve greeted Diamond at the door. Her eyes glistened with excitement. For a moment, Diamond could imagine her mother at her age: young, beautiful, vibrant, full of passion. This closeness with her mother warmed her heart.

They hugged, then Genevieve pulled Diamond into the living room. "My goodness, girl. I had no idea that Jackson Wright was such a handsome man!"

"Isn't he?"

"You know, in some ways he reminds me of how your father was when I met him—confident, borderline arrogant, self-assured, intelligent as all get-out and handsome. Baby, couldn't nobody bless a suit the way your father could!"

"And I remember the story. You said you knew right away that Dad was the one."

"As soon as I laid eyes on that lanky joker, yes, sir." Genevieve's eyes sparkled with memories.

"Mom, I've never felt about anyone the way I do Jackson. I thought I knew love with Benjamin but—" Diamond shook her head "—now I know that there are levels to loving, and what I feel now…I've never felt before."

"I felt the same way about your father," Genevieve said as she poured tea. She handed a cup to Diamond. "At just the thought of Donald Drake, at the mention of his name, my heart would beat faster. Still does." Genevieve put a hand on Diamond's arm. "When the information regarding Jackson's past came to your father, I was quite concerned. But after meeting him and seeing the way he looks at you…Diamond, I think he just might be the one."

"Really, Mom, you think so?"

Genevieve nodded.

These words made Diamond's heart soar. "So you were watching him, right? How does he look at me?"

"Diamond, baby, he looks at you like your father looks at me…with eyes full of love."

# Chapter 30

The next three weeks passed by in a whirlwind of love, work and bottles of Drake premier wine. Both were busy, but Diamond and Jackson still managed to spend quality time together. They carved it out where they could find it, like now, the day before the resort's grand opening. Earlier, the family and Drake Wine employees had toured the new facility. Their wide eyes and gape-mouthed expressions told Jackson of the bang-up job he and Boss Construction had done better than words ever could. Donald Drake couldn't have been more impressed at what Jackson had pulled off in so little time. The only other time he'd seen quality work performed this fast was when Ty Pennington was screaming into his bullhorn and telling another family "Welcome home!" The thirty-room hotel was fully booked for the holiday weekend, and largely due to a lineup of R & B classic artists and smooth jazz favorites, their Sunday "Brunch & Beats" was sold out through Valentine's Day.

Diamond looked at her watch. She couldn't believe it was ten o'clock and she was still working. Kathleen had left just moments before. Everyone was tired. *This time tomorrow, it'll be done. Drake Wines Resort & Spa will be officially opened for business.* The day after that, Thanksgiving, her family had planned a private celebration. Diamond couldn't wait.

Placing her keys in her hand, she reached for the door and gasped as a tall, hulking figure blocked the path in front of her. "Jackson! Baby! You scared me half to death!"

Jackson pulled her into his embrace. "What are you still doing here, baby? Where's security? I don't like the idea of you being out here alone." While not sharing everything with Donald and her brothers, he had mentioned that there were people who'd like nothing better than to cause him problems, and with their relationship becoming public, Diamond may be targeted, as well.

"Phillip is probably making his rounds," she said, pulling out her cell phone. "But I'm going to call Donovan nonetheless, make sure that the extra security are on the premises."

After placing the call, she turned to Jackson. "Now, Mr. Wright, let me ask you the same question. What are you doing here this late? I'm sure you're exhausted. Your men have been working around the clock. And the hard work has paid off. I've said it a thousand times and I'll say it again—the place looks amazing."

"Thank you, love." He took her hand and walked them to the side of the building where the carts were parked. "Get in," he told her, reaching beneath the seat to where he now knew they kept the keys.

"Where are we going?" Diamond asked, even as a wave of excitement surged through her.

"This will be our last night with the place all to ourselves. We're going to go and christen the Papa Dee Suite."

"Wait. I'll be right back." Diamond went into the office. "Let's stop by the rack," she said. They did, and shortly after entering the warehouse, Diamond returned with a chilled bottle of sparkling wine, a vintage bottle from another great year. The two were silent as Jackson expertly navigated the cart up the winding road that led to the old house. The night was cool, the moon was full and the stars twinkled like so many diamonds in the sky. Jackson turned the cart onto the pine-tree-lined entrance that now welcomed guests. Small lights twinkled from the boughs, creating a magical ambience around the freshly painted white house that beckoned in the distance. The house had been expertly lifted and now sat on a large expanse of smooth stone. The original porch had been refortified and expanded to the length of the front of the house. As a nod to its history, a lone plank remained loose, with a key inside.

Diamond smiled as she retrieved the key to the newly installed mahogany door outfitted with beveled glass, a single rose etched into the design. They entered and were immediately enveloped with the energy of the remodeled home, now with gleaming hardwood floors, floral silk-covered walls and a fireplace where wood sat stacked ready for use. The downstairs had stayed true to the original design, but upstairs the transformation had been more striking. A wall had been removed to turn the entire upstairs into a master suite, add a walk-in closet and an en suite bath with every amenity. A gas fireplace now anchored the upstairs area. Jackson walked over and turned it on, while Diamond tried out the stereo system, prestocked with thousands of tunes in every genre. The mood set, Jackson walked to the table where Diamond had placed the bubbly, popped the cork and filled their flutes.

"To an amazing woman," he said, his eyes shining with

love for her, "who knows who I am, where I've been, and accepts every part of me. I love you, Diamond."

"I love you, too."

They drank as the nostalgic sounds of John Coltrane's "Naima" set the mood—sultry and soulful, melodic and hot. Dancing around the room, they drank not only the sparkling vintage but the love that was pouring from each other's eyes. "I want to ask you something," Jackson said, grinding his already hardening manhood into Diamond's soft flesh.

"Yes?" Her whisper was filled with notes that suggested that at any moment he could have asked her to run down the I-15 buck naked and she would have obliged.

"Are you seeing anyone else?"

Diamond stopped moving. "Where did that come from?"

"From my wanting to know. Is there anyone else in your life right now?"

Diamond laid her head back on Jackson's shoulder and resumed their slow groove. "No. What about you?"

"No one." Silky notes dribbled from Coltrane's sax into the room, making them giddy, like the bubbly, like each other. "I was tested six months ago and always practice safe sex. But I believe what I have with you is special, Diamond. We did it the other night by accident, but from now on out, when we make love, I don't want anything between us."

The thought of her and Jackson in the raw, flesh to flesh, made Diamond tingle all over. It brought back memories of the lone other night where it had been so, when she'd poured out her love and he'd emptied his heart by sharing his past. She closed her eyes as he kissed her temple, sure that he could detect the rapidity of her heartbeat. "I'm on the Pill," she said at last, having started back on them six months ago to help lessen her cramps and regulate her periods. "I want to feel you, too."

As Coltrane's sax slid into Thelonious Monk's piano—

and in between hot and sticky kisses—Jackson and Diamond undressed. They walked to the glass, steel and mosaic stone shower. Diamond smiled as she reached for the cellophane-wrapped sponge, remembering Jackson's response when she commented on their proliferation for shower-taking. "I like tasting you all over, baby. And I don't like to fake the funk... or lick it." They'd showered, and then Jackson had shown her exactly what he'd meant.

Jackson took it from her. "Here, let me."

He opened the liquid soap, poured a generous amount on the sponge and took special pains as he tended to Diamond's neck, shoulders, back and butt with kisses on the same. "Spread your legs, baby." He washed her tenderly, lovingly before his tongue replaced the sponge. He dipped his tongue in her feminine flower, lapped her juices like the sweetest nectar until the musky odor of their abiding affection filled the room, along with Diamond's mewling and traces of "'Round Midnight." He finished washing her down to her toes, and then she returned the favor. When she came to the massive weapon that would soon be inside her, she stroked it lovingly, circling the perfectly shaped mushroom tip with her finger and following it with her tongue. Grabbing Jackson's hard, round buttocks, she took him in, licking, sucking, setting up a rhythm that almost took her man over the edge. He took her hand, but instead of the bed, he picked her up and walked them to the wall. Her legs instinctively circled his waist, and when they did, she was an open target and his sword was poised for the sweet attack. With one long thrust, he joined them together, squeezing her cheeks, stroking her sensitive entrance, branding her body with his dick. Balancing her against the wall, he took hold of her hips and took their dance to yet another level. Every time Diamond thought it couldn't get any better, he surprised her. By rotating his hips to a groove of his own, he touched every part of Diamond's essence and every fiber of her soul. Just before her release, he stopped, led her to the edge of the bed and guided her to her knees. There, once again, he took a loving hold of her hips, teasing her with his tip, kissing her shoulders, back, buttocks, thighs, kissing her as if she were ambrosia. "I love you, Diamond," he whispered, as with quick, sure strokes he guided himself inside her. "I love the feel of you, my love." He settled in deep and leaned over. "Do you like this, baby? Do you like the feel of me inside you?" Diamond nodded, but when she didn't answer audibly he pulled out and slowly pushed in again. "Do you like this?"

"Yes," Diamond stuttered, grinding herself against him, taking him deeper still.

"What about this?" he asked, moving in and out and side to side, then becoming still again. He reached around, tweaked her nipples and then, without warning, drove himself deeply inside her with such an intensity, such ferocity, that Diamond felt as intense of a release as she'd ever felt start at her core that straightened her hair and curled her toes. She'd never been a screamer and was therefore surprised to learn the high C bouncing off the walls was not the stereo but her own voice.

"Jackson!"

Her shout sent him over the edge, and then he joined her on the bed. He cuddled her close, feeling a contentment he hadn't thought possible, no longer able to imagine life without this jewel he'd found. "You make me happy, baby," he whispered in her ear.

"And you make me work," she replied.

He chuckled. "What?"

"That's right. Because of you, I have to call housekeeping for a late-night cleanup."

"Oh! What just happened is my fault then, huh?"

"Absolutely." She turned to face him. "And I enjoyed every

delicious minute of it. I think Nicodemus would have liked you and would be glad to know that the home has once again been christened by a Drake."

# Chapter 31

Jackson walked into the office carrying flowers and a blue box. Marissa looked up in wonder, not so much that her boss had bought flowers. He often surprised her with such thoughtful treats. No, it was the fact that he was humming that caught her off guard.

"What happened to you?" she asked, her dimple twinkling as she spoke. "Are those gifts for me or the woman who put that smile on your face and that pep in your step?"

"These flowers are for the best assistant in the world," he said. "I appreciate you postponing your trip home to help with these last-minute details of the Drake opening. This," he said, placing the Tiffany box on the desk, "is for you to wear to the opening tonight."

"Me? Boss, you know I don't do those fancy-smancy gatherings."

"You'll like this one. The place is really beautiful, the

Drakes are good people and Diamond has two brothers. Both are handsome and available."

"Diamond Drake? That's who has you smiling like you're auditioning for a toothpaste commercial? I know what you're trying to do, Jackson. And I appreciate it. But my flight leaves first thing in the morning. And Thanksgiving is the busiest travel holiday of the year. I still need to pack and—"

"I'm sorry. Did I form that as a question? I meant to say that part of your job requirement is that you attend the grand opening of Drake Wines Resort & Spa."

Marissa huffed, but in actuality she was only mildly annoyed. In the past year, a so-called friend and a betrayed trust had sent her reeling. Jackson and this job had been a lifeline. If not for this anchor, she would have drowned. "Why would they open the day before Thanksgiving anyway?" she said, reaching for the famous blue box. "I'm sure their workers would rather be with their families."

"Their rationale is that oftentimes those without families are forgotten. Not everyone has a home to go to, and not everyone has a family that they're dying to see. The fact that both the restaurant and hotel are sold out is proof enough that their choice was a good one."

Marissa opened the box and pulled out a beautiful watch: functional yet elegant at the same time. "This is beautiful, Jackson. But really…it's too much."

"Does that mean I can skip your raise this year?"

Marissa hurriedly put the watch back in the box and pushed it toward Jackson. "Don't get it twisted, Boss. I'd rather put my money in the bank than wear it on my arm."

"Ha!"

"Thank you, Jackson. We have a lot to be thankful for."

"No more letters?"

Marissa shook her head. "Not for almost three weeks. A couple hang-ups but that could be anyone. I think the beefed-up security since the break-in and the very obvious cameras around the place have scared off whoever this was."

"I hope you're right. In the meantime, we have an opening to attend. Why don't you ride with me? You can take off now, and I'll pick you up in a couple hours."

Marissa reached for her purse. "When it comes to getting off early, you don't have to ask me twice. I'll see you soon!"

Jackson left her area and walked around the office. It mostly resembled a ghost town, but he saw one lone light shining at the back of the office. He walked in. It was his newest employee, a junior architect he'd recently recruited from the East Coast.

"Carlton? Are you kidding me?" Jackson stepped into his office. "What are you doing here? I thought you'd be chilling with your folks in D.C. by now."

"Hey, Boss. Getting it in, I guess. You know how we do."

"I appreciate the dedication and all but working through Thanksgiving? That's not required, bro."

"I guess it's my Type A personality. I'm almost done with this set of sketches. They're for the Chicago job. Another hour and then I'm out. Catching a nine o'clock red-eye."

"That's what's up. You have a good one, man."

"You, too."

Jackson continued down the hall to his office. As soon as he made sure everything was locked up tight, he left the Boss Construction offices and headed for the elevator. Just as he reached it, his phone rang. "Jackson."

"Sorry to bother you, Jackson. This is Frank."

"Happy holidays, man."

Frank continued in his no-nonsense style. "I've got news."

Normalcy continued around him, but Jackson's body went on high alert. "Today?"

"Evil doesn't pause for the holidays."

"Talk."

"A childhood friend of yours has been snooping around, asking questions. We finally got one of the neighborhood know-it-alls to talk."

"I thought I told you that I didn't want you digging into my childhood."

"Yeah, well, call me hardheaded. My wife sure does. I had a hunch, Jackson, and it wouldn't go away. When all the investigative roads kept leading back to Brandon Dent, I homed in on his prison connections. I learned the identity of Slim Shady."

"It's not Marshall Mathers?" Jackson asked, his mind once again going to the only Slim Shady he knew of…hip-hop's well-known White rap artist.

"No, Marshall isn't the name I came up with."

Obviously Frank didn't get the joke. "Who is it, then?"

"Shay Thomas." Complete silence as Jackson processed this news. "Name ring a bell?"

"Yes," Jackson said after slowly releasing a breath. "He was one of my best friends from back in the day."

"Did you know he went to prison?"

Jackson closed his eyes against the memories. "Yes."

"Word on the street is he blames you for the bid he did." He was silent as he imagined a myriad of emotions playing across Jackson's face. "Do you have any idea what he's talking about? What crime he committed that you know about and why he'd want to do you harm?"

"Yes."

"And it never crossed your mind that telling me about this might be a good idea?"

"I didn't think it was necessary. Shay and I were best friends. He knows I had nothing to do with why he's in prison. That he might be the person behind the threats never crossed my mind."

Frank then said, "Shay was released from prison a couple

months ago. Went back to the neighborhood and started asking about you. Says you broke a confidence and it's time for payback. He saw an article on you in a magazine, Jackson. So he knows where you work and maybe even where you live. You need to watch your back, be careful of your surroundings until we get to the bottom of this."

They ended the call, and Jackson proceeded to his car. While driving home to change for the opening, his mind whirled, his entire body was tense. *My boy Shay is free? And saying I broke a confidence? What the hell is he talking about?* Jackson recalled the last time he saw his former best friend, whom they used to call Toe-2-Toe for the way he liked to fistfight. It was the return back to the neighborhood for his sixteenth birthday. He hadn't seen his childhood friends for two years, and by the time he returned, hoping to reestablish a connection, Shay and Jackson's other best friend, Wesley "Glock" Adams, were deep into gang activity. Shay, one year older than Jackson, was already a major dealer. One particular night, amid the haze of alcohol and weed, Shay had confided to his friends that he'd been threatened by a rival gang member who wanted his clientele. Shay vowed to do whatever it took to protect his gravy train. They rode around most of the night, drinking and smoking. Jackson, who hadn't ever consumed this level of alcohol and weed in one sitting, fell asleep in the backseat. That's why he didn't hear Shay and Wesley plan a robbery at a gas station in the rival gang's territory, believing that the gang member who'd threatened him would get pinned with the crime. Nor was he aware when they pulled up to a convenience store and pulled a gun on the lone Middle Eastern man behind the counter. The man resisted by pulling a weapon from under the counter, but his thirty-eight-caliber handgun was no match for the 10mm Glock that Shay carried. The convenience store owner was killed; the three boys were arrested. But thanks to an outstanding lawyer who convinced the judge and prosecuting attorneys that Jackson had no knowledge of or involvement in the crime, he was released without standing trial. And thanks to his uncle John's influence, his court records were eventually expunged. Shay and Wesley were found guilty of murder in the first degree, and a year after that, Wesley was killed in a prison fight. This news, along with learning that Uncle John wanted to someday turn the construction company over to him, was the catalyst to changing the direction of Jackson's life. He got in with a new crowd in suburban San Diego, young men who wanted legitimate success. With his former best friends gone and his mother in prison, his old neighborhood no longer held any type of attraction. He never returned.

But one thing was certain, Jackson thought as he pulled out his phone and dialed a number. It was time to go back now.

# Chapter 32

When Jackson and Marissa arrived at Drake Wines Resort & Spa, the party was already in full swing. He left the car with the valet, and admired the thoughtful landscaping, which included palm trees, colorful rows of bird-of-paradise, red amaranth and other colorful flowers. Inside they were greeted by sleek slate flooring, floor-to-ceiling windows and glistening chandeliers. Jackson noted Taylor's final touches to the canvas he'd created as they walked through the packed dining room and over to where the Drake siblings were standing. He did not, however, pick up on the pair of eyes that were watching him.

"Hello, everyone," Jackson said, after giving Diamond a quick hug and squeeze. "I'd like to introduce my assistant, Marissa Hayes. Marissa, this is Dexter Drake."

"Um, pleased to meet you," the ever-flirtatious Dexter drawled.

"The eldest in the clan, Donovan."

"A pleasure," Donovan said, shaking her hand and placing the other one lightly on her arm. They touched, and a bolt as powerful as an electrical current passed between them. Marissa quickly pulled back her hand and diverted her eyes. Donovan's eyes narrowed as he noted her unease. An unexplainable urge arose within him—the desire to see a smile on that beautifully chocolate, dimpled face.

"And this is Diamond."

Diamond leaned forward for a light hug.

"I've heard so much about you," Marissa said, still feeling the tingles from Donovan's handshake. "You're even more beautiful than Jackson described."

"That's more than I can say. Jackson," Diamond teased, "why didn't you tell me you had *America's Next Top Model* working in your office?"

"My bad," Jackson replied, with hand over heart. "And the thing is, she's as beautiful on the inside as she is on the outside."

"Well, welcome to Drake Wines Resort & Spa," Diamond concluded. "Take the tour, taste the food and enjoy the wine. I'm going to steal your boss for a minute. Enjoy." Diamond reached for Jackson's hand and led them away from the crowd. "Okay, out with it," she said when they were alone.

"Out with what?"

"Don't even try it, Jackson. Something's wrong. I see it in your eyes."

It took effort, but Jackson summoned a smile. Maybe nothing would come of the phone call he made earlier; maybe Shay's return to their old neighborhood was a one-time thing. "Nothing for you to worry your pretty little head about, princess."

"Oh, quit it already with the 'princess' routine. Contrary to your misguided belief, I'm not a China doll who will run fleeing at the first sign of trouble. You ought to know that by now." Diamond continued to stare at Jackson. "This has to do with what happened at your office, doesn't it? Do you know who did it? Did they catch the guy?" She rose to her full height—which in her three-inch heels was almost six feet—full of spunk and attitude. Jackson had no doubt that if the culprit walked into the room she'd kick butt now and ask questions later!

Jackson didn't have to try and smile this time. "Dang, baby. When they do catch him, he'd better stay out of your way!"

"That's right," she said, relaxing her stance. "Don't even try and mess with my man."

Jackson's smile widened. "Hum…I like the sound of that."

Donald and Genevieve approached them, looking like royalty in black tux and sparkling forest-green gown.

The two men shook hands. "All of wine country has turned out to view your handiwork," Donald said to Jackson. "I think your business in this area is getting ready to pick up considerably."

"Thank you, sir. We're already booked solid for the next six months. The new customers will have to get in line."

"That's a good problem to have."

Jackson turned to Genevieve and placed a kiss on her cheek. "Mrs. Drake, you look lovely."

Genevieve smiled appreciatively as her gaze swept six feet five inches of perfection. "You clean up pretty well yourself," she said. "You look almost as good as your handiwork." She swept her hand up to the ceiling where the sun shone brightly through the glass ceiling. "This ceiling is one of my favorite features. It's absolutely stunning."

"Almost as stunning as you," Jackson replied, with a twinkle in his eye.

"Careful, Jackson," Donald said. "That's a married woman you're flirting around with."

Diamond laughed. "Dad!"

The four continued to share small talk until Jackson felt his phone vibrate against his waist. He pulled it out and looked at the caller ID. "Excuse me." After walking a short distance away, he answered the call. "Blade! Happy Thanksgiving, man."

"Happy Thanksgiving, stranger!" Sonny "Blade" Wilkins was one of the best barbers on the West Coast and the Mayor of Crenshaw Boulevard. His nickname came from the way he could carve hair into letters, pictures and more using a single-edged razor blade. He'd been around as long as Jackson had been alive. Very little happened in or around the neighborhood that Blade didn't know about. "When I got your message I just about keeled over dead!" A rumbling laughter followed this comment.

Jackson didn't realize until then how long it had been since he'd heard the sound and how much he'd missed it. "It has been a long time. I wasn't even sure your number would work."

"I don't know why you'd think that," Blade replied in mock indignation. "I been on the block for almost forty years. Ain't going nowhere."

"It's good to talk to you, Blade. What's shakin', man?"

"Nothing much except the leaves in the trees. What's up with you, Boss? Living so high on the hog that you can't come and visit the chittlins every once in a while?"

"Ha! I apologize, man, been busy."

"Trust me, I know how it is when you become one of those corporate executives…forget about the little people."

"Man, you need to stop."

"You know I'm just messin' with you, son. How you livin…besides large?"

"I'm blessed, man, no complaints."

"How's your mama?"

Jackson immediately ridged. "How am I supposed to know?"

Blade's pause conveyed his displeasure. But his tone was calm, almost fatherly, when he continued. "She may not have been the best mother, but boy, she's the only one you've got. You have been to see her, haven't you?"

Jackson sighed. "Not for a while."

"Why not?"

Jackson gave Blade the condensed version of his last prison visit with Sharon Burnett. "It hurts me more to be around her than to be away," he finished, vulnerability coating every word he spoke. "I don't need to be reminded of my life back then, or that she loves others more than me."

There was a long pause before Blade answered. "Now, lookie here, son. I need you to listen to me. As bad as it was, your mother did the best she could in raising you. I knew her mother, your grandmother, and I can tell you something. Life for neither one of those women was easy." Blade was unaware of the sheen of tears that covered Jackson's eyes before being rapidly blinked away. "You have nothing to be ashamed of, not about your mother or your past. In fact, where you've been and where you are now should fill you with pride. Don't you see it, Boss? Your story reads like the American dream. You can use what happened to you as an example to other young men out here in the street. You hear me?"

It came slowly, but finally Jackson answered. "Thanks for saying that, Blade." It wasn't the first time he'd heard such words. He and Uncle John had had a similar conversation shortly after Jackson had moved in. But hearing them from another father-figure whom he deeply respected gave the words new meaning. Now, in adulthood, they made sense. In that simple yet profound moment something shifted, and for the first time Jackson considered not hiding his past, but using it to help others. And he also thought about once again visiting his mom.

"All right, enough of me playing Dr. Phil," Blade said to lighten the mood. Jackson could hear something being poured in the background. "What can I do for you?"

"I'm looking for some information, and I'd like to keep the fact that I'm asking around confidential."

"I can do that."

"I heard that Shay is out of prison."

"I heard that, too. Haven't seen him though."

Jackson rubbed his chin as he pondered this info. Back in the day, Shay, Wesley and Jackson practically lived at Blade's Barbershop. For them, Blade was almost like the father none of them had had. If back in the neighborhood, Jackson would have thought that one of Shay's first stops out of the joint. "Will you do me a favor and let me know if you see him?"

"Why do I get the feeling that this isn't about sharing a beer and talking about old times?"

Jackson barely hesitated before coming clean with Blade. He figured the more the old man knew, the better his chances of getting the info he needed. He shared the short version of the story. "Someone broke into our offices and, uh, damaged some equipment…among other things," Jackson finished.

"Ah, so that's why you thought of Shay." Both men knew that Shay could pick a lock faster than most folk could use a key.

"To tell the truth, Shay never crossed my mind. I'd been focused on a past employee, somebody mad because they were out of a job. It wasn't him, but turns out his nephew had lived life on the other side of the law and knew Shay. The investigator on this case started snooping around and found out that Shay, who has gone from Toe-2-Toe to Slim Shady by the way, was released a little before the first letter arrived. It's a long shot because I don't know what kind of

beef Shay would have with me." Again, Jackson's mind went
to the crime that had sent Shay and Wesley to prison. But
Shay knew why Jackson hadn't gotten prison time. He was
innocent of any wrongdoing!

"If I see him, do you want me to try and find out for you?"

"I'd appreciate it."

"If he asks, should I give him your number?"

*Keep your friends close and your enemies closer.* "Yes."

Jackson ended the call and rejoined the party. He joked
with Diamond's brothers and mingled with guests. The wine
flowed and the evening passed and Jackson almost forgot that
he had a problem. Until around ten o'clock, when he received
a text from Blade:

Walked the neighborhood and ran into Shay. He
asked about where you were. Wouldn't tell me why
he wanted to see you. Didn't feel good, Jackson. I
think ur right to keep an eye on ur boy.

# *Chapter 33*

Thanksgiving with the Drakes was a splendid affair. They'd spent it holed up in their estate and, except for one call from the hotel's general manager, had been able to enjoy the holiday much like the rest of America—work free. Jackson had joined them, as had Dexter's latest love interest. But now, at the end of the evening, it was just the family.

"What happened to Jackson?" Dexter asked, as he reached for a handful of nuts before taking a seat. The family had retired to the great room—ties loose, shoes off, nightcaps in hand.

"Something came up," Diamond replied, a slight scowl on her face. He'd acted strangely all evening. To say she was concerned was an understatement.

"He is a very handsome man," Genevieve commented.

"With a very attractive bank account," the ever money-conscious Donovan added. "That never hurts to help a man look good."

"Much better than that Benjamin joker," Donald said, casually swirling a tumbler of vintage cognac. "That man was a leech if ever I saw one. Sorry, baby, but you know I never totally trusted your ex. And that's the truth."

"What counts is a man's character, heart and integrity. Those are the reasons I'm dating Jackson."

"Sounds like wedding bells to me," Dexter said. "When's the date, sister?"

"Both of y'all need to get out of my business and focus on your own. Donovan, you're the oldest. You should be married with children by now. And you," Diamond said, as she pointed a manicured finger at Dexter, "need to quit playing the field like you're Michael Vick at the Superbowl and choose a wifey."

"Whoa! Not so fast, sister. I'm the baby boy with more wild oats to sow."

"Dexter," Genevieve chided.

"Sorry, Mom, but you know what I mean. I probably won't get married until I'm forty years old."

"At which time your mom and I will be pushing, what, seventy?" Donald queried. "Thanks a lot."

Genevieve's back straightened as she looked around the room. "Listen, you three. I'm all for being selective when it comes to choosing one's mate, but it is time we expanded this family and ensured the legacy. I believe that I've been more than patient when it comes to my desire of being a grandmother. But my patience is running thin. Y'all better get on it!"

"Did Miss Proper English just say 'y'all'? Mama, you'd better make that your last glass of wine!"

Genevieve laughed. "I guess I am a little tipsy."

"And I'm a little tired," Donald said, standing. "Wife, let's go to bed."

"What time does your plane leave tomorrow?"

"At 9:00 a.m." Donald and Genevieve were joining two other couples for a mini-vacation in Cabo San Lucas. "Good night, all."

The three siblings hugged their parents and then settled back onto the couch and chair, watching their parents hold hands as they left the room.

"I hope I can have a love like that," Diamond said with a sigh.

"If that's going to happen," Dexter said, "you need to find out what's going on with your boy."

"Why, what did you notice?" *I thought I was the only one who detected his jumpy mood.*

"I don't know, but when he and that fine assistant—"

"That fine, *aloof* assistant," Donovan interjected with a scowl.

"Her name is Marissa," Diamond offered.

"When he and that fine, aloof Marissa were waiting for the valet they were in conversation and it looked pretty intense."

Diamond's interest was immediately piqued. "Did you hear anything?"

Dexter shook his head. "Wasn't close enough to hear what they were saying but from the look on your boy's face, he wasn't too happy."

Jackson exited the 10 Freeway onto Crenshaw Boulevard. How long had it been since he'd seen these streets? Ten years? Fifteen? He couldn't remember. After leaving the party, he'd traded his tailored suit for jeans and a T-shirt, and stopped the Maserati for his old faithful Jeep to blend in with the Crenshaw cruisers. Memories assailed him as he passed restaurants and wig shops, the Angeles Funeral Home and the West Angeles Church of God In Christ that he'd attended once or twice as a child. He reached Leimert Park, passed Blade's Barbershop and continued on a few blocks before pulling up in front of the well-kept lawn of a small residence. He parked the Jeep and looked around as he bounded the steps. The street was quiet, but there was a chill in the air.

"Hey, Jackson. Good to see you, son."

"You, too, Blade," Jackson said, as he hugged the older gentleman, who seemed not to age. The barber's slight body was still as wiry as Jackson remembered, his bald head perfectly round, his face free of wrinkles. "The neighborhood hasn't changed much."

"The more things change, the more they stay the same." Blade eyed Jackson a long moment. "I don't know if it was a good idea for you to come down here. I told you that when Shay asked about you, it didn't seem like good was on his mind."

"Good was rarely on Shay's mind," Jackson responded. "Sounds like what you said is right. The more things change, the more they stay the same."

Both men were quiet a moment, lost in their thoughts. Then Blade looked at Jackson with narrowed eyes. "Do you think this has something to do with the botched robbery, with why Shay went to jail?"

"That's what I've thought," Jackson responded as he paced the room. "But why would he have a beef against me for something that was his own damn fault? I was passed out in the backseat and didn't even hear them planning the crime. Didn't wake up until I heard gunshots, followed by Shay and Wesley racing to the car and us spending the next fifteen minutes trying to outrun the police." Jackson stopped pacing, placed his hands on his hips. "So Shay came into the shop specifically to ask about me?"

"No, I ran into him, standing on over there by Eso Won Books. All buff and whatnot, you know how they pump iron behind bars. Looks good, though, for someone who's just spent the last fifteen years in prison."

"Where is he?" Jackson asked, heading to the door.

"Hold up now, son," Blade said, walking to and standing in front of the door. "You've got too much going for you to tangle with Shay. If he wants to hurt you, he has much less to lose."

"I'm not going to spend the rest of my life looking behind my back or over my shoulder, Blade. I no longer live in the hood but I've never backed down from somebody wanting to bring it. And I'm sure as hell not going to start now."

# Chapter 34

"I don't like the sound of this, Jackson," Diamond said, pacing her office much as Jackson had done in Blade's house last night. She shifted the phone to her other ear, sat and immediately stood back up to pace again.

"Don't worry about it, baby girl. I can take care of myself."

"No doubt, but why did you feel the need to go back to your old neighborhood and stir things up? What if this Shay character comes after you?"

"Baby, there's a different code of ethics in the streets. You can't have people thinking you're afraid of them. All I did was go to a couple spots and spread the word that I'm not hiding and I'm not running."

Diamond snorted. "Men! You and your pissing contests."

"Shay has always been a lot of talk and little action. I'll be okay."

Diamond's tone turned sultry. "I want to see you. You ran away from me last night."

"I want to see you, too, baby. But I forgot something at the office. Came back to get it and am now going over some plans one of my architects left for me."

"But it's the holiday weekend, baby! We're supposed to be eating leftover turkey and watching classic DVDs."

"I'll be leaving here around four, five o'clock. I'll call you then."

"Sounds like a plan. I love you."

"I love you, too, Diamond."

Diamond spent the day with her grandparents and Papa Dee. At three o'clock, she took a shower, packed a bag for the weekend and headed downstairs.

"Going somewhere, little sister?" Dexter asked as he made himself a turkey salad sandwich.

Diamond picked a chip off of his plate. "He doesn't know it yet but I'm taking advantage of the fact that my watchdogs, otherwise known as Donald and Genevieve, are out of town. I'm spending the weekend with Jackson. He works too hard and I want to remind him that there are more important things in life than running a business."

Dexter laughed. "You're one to talk. I think you're more driven than me or Donovan."

"Hey, I've got to hold my own!"

"Oh, you're holding your own all right. And then some! So you're headed to that fancy estate you told me about?"

"He's at work. I'm going to surprise him there. What are you doing?"

"I'm headed to San Diego myself, to Donovan's house."

"He's actually going to spend some time there?"

"Yep, got a poker game all set up. Time for some male bonding."

Diamond hugged her brother. "You guys have fun. I love you."

Dexter hugged her back. "I love you, too."

About an hour later, Diamond pulled up in front of a tall office building in downtown San Diego. After a quick check of her makeup she exited the car and entered the empty lobby, looking for her phone where she'd stored the elevator access code that would take her to the Boss Construction offices located on the top two floors. She scrolled through her memos. *Ah, here it is.* She keyed in the code, and with it being the Friday after a holiday and the place empty, the elevator door opened almost immediately. She stepped in, turned around— and looked into a pair of the coldest eyes she'd ever seen.

"Oh," she exclaimed, as her hand went to her throat. "I didn't hear you behind me."

"I know." The stranger smiled. His teeth were straight and white and set in a handsome face. The smile didn't reach his eyes.

A chill went down her back. *Danger, Will Robinson! Danger, Will Robinson!* If theirs had been a public company, she would have bet her shares of Drake Wine stock that she was staring into the reason that Jackson was jumpy last night.

Instinct took over. "Darn it, I forgot my phone." She stepped toward the door just as it was about to close. And felt a strong hand wrap itself around her arm.

"Not so fast, pretty lady. I think you need to take this ride with me."

"Oh, thank you," Diamond said, offering as big a smile as you can muster when about to pee your pants. "But I'm seeing someone."

"Let me guess. Jackson *Boss* Wright?" He sneered as if something profane had just been said.

Charm hadn't worked, so she tried bravado. Attitude replaced the smile. The stranger's grip felt like steel. "You really need to let go of my arm."

"Okay." He shoved her back against the elevator wall. "Go ahead and key in the code that will take us to the penthouse. I know that's where you're headed. I've been following your boy for days, was even at y'all's bougie-ass hotel the day it opened." Diamond's eyes widened. "That's right," the stranger proudly continued. "I've been biding my time, waiting for just the right moment, and since seeing old boy's ride in the garage, I've been waiting almost three hours for somebody to come help me get up in this bitch. So, with all this waiting I've been doing, you might not want to try my patience."

Call her crazy, but Diamond didn't think this guy wanted to go to Jackson's office to sing "Kumbaya." Again she lunged toward the door. An arm wrapped around her waist, slammed her against an equally hard chest. She squirmed, kicked, tried to bite. It would take the Jaws of Life to free her.

"Go ahead. Try and get away. I like my women feisty."

Diamond froze. She didn't want to appeal to any part of this man. *Be calm. Think! Don't let him know you're scared. Shitless.* "I hope you like them stubborn, too. Because if you're waiting for me to start this elevator, we'll be here all night."

Diamond blinked, and there was a gun in her face.

"You've obviously got me confused with your punk-ass boyfriend upstairs. I'm tired of playing with you. Start the elevator." He pressed the muzzle of the gun against her temple. "Now!"

"I don't have it, the code, I don't have it." The man grabbed her hair. "Really! I swear. I've only been here once and I called Jackson to get in. The phone is there." A shaky finger pointed to a box on the wall.

The stranger's eyes narrowed. "Pick it up," he finally said, with a slight lift of his head. "Call your man. I'll be listening, so don't try anything foolish. Or else there'll be two people dying tonight."

Diamond swallowed, willed her nerves to stop jumping.

She squeezed the receiver against her ear. Jackson answered, and her heartbeat went into overdrive.

"Hey, baby."

"Diamond?"

"Who else, fool? And don't even think about not buzzing me up there. I don't care how pissed off you are about the note I left turning your ass down last night."

Long pause. Diamond imagined Jackson looking at the phone as if it had sprouted horns. *Note, note, the threatening note.* Diamond thought with all of her might, trying to send a telepathic warning. *I've never written you a note in my life. Think, Jackson. Who's been sending you notes!*

He didn't get the memo.

The elevator began its rise to the top floor. Diamond's heart dropped to her feet. A myriad of thoughts and escape scenarios raced across her brain. Would Jackson meet her at the elevator door or be in his office? Should she try and run in the other direction…divert the attention away from him? Then she thought of the gun—the sneer on the face of the man who held it, the hatred she saw in his eyes. No, this wasn't the day to take a bullet. Unfortunately for her she'd forgone a bulletproof vest for the more everyday Baby Phat top with skinny jeans.

She looked at the numbers: 20, 21, 22… *Think, Diamond! You have got to do something!* She took a step away from the stranger. And the gun.

He stepped right with her. "Try anything and I'll drop you like a bad habit," he said, his tone deceptively soft. "Think I'm playing? Just try me."

"Can I at least put my keys away? I locked myself out of the car once. Jackson knows it's the first thing I do now, put my keys in my purse."

The stranger adopted a wide-legged stance, trained the gun directly at Diamond's chest. "Like a bad habit," he drawled.

Diamond placed the keys inside her purse, pushing a button on her phone in the process. *Thank God my hands-free is still plugged into the phone. We won't hear whoever answers.* Thankful, too, that she watched the occasional crime show. She forced herself to look at the stranger, took in smooth brown skin, the mole on the right side of his face, just above his mustache, and a tattoo partially visible at the neckline of his tee. If they needed an artist sketch later, she was their girl.

"Who are you?" she asked, careful to talk loud enough to be heard through the leather of her purse.

The stranger gave her the once-over. "You'll find out soon enough. And who knows. Once I've handled my business with Boss I just might—" he licked his lips "—handle my business with you."

Diamond knew that she'd use every ounce of fight inside her to not be assaulted by this man. Her mind went into overdrive. *Who did I call last? Whoever it was...please pick up!*

# Chapter 35

Several men sat in Donovan's luxuriously appointed, state-of-the-art game room. Six of them were around a mahogany game table playing poker. Dexter had just given up his hand to take a call from his flavor of the month, who'd joined the family at yesterday's dinner. "Hold on, baby. This is my sister on the other line. Hello?"

"Does handling your business with Jackson involve using that gun?"

Dexter's brow furrowed as he looked at his phone. "Diamond?"

"Don't worry about my business with your boy. Just chill and you might not get hurt."

Diamond raised her voice. "Do I look stupid to you? Do *you* think that *I* think you're going to commit a crime and leave a witness? Murdering the owner of San Diego's top construction company, in his swanky penthouse offices no less? This is going to be all over the news. You'll never get away."

Dexter stepped back into the game room. "Don. Come check this out, man."

One look at his brother's face and Donovan knew whatever was happening was serious. "Excuse me, fellas." He walked over to Dexter, who quickly led them out of the room, down the hall and into a bedroom where he closed the door.

"What's up?"

"Shh." Dexter pushed the speaker button. "Listen."

They reached the top floor. The stranger placed Diamond in front of him and put the gun to her head. "I'm warning you. Don't try nothin'," he growled, pushing the hard steel against her head for emphasis. "I'll shoot your fine ass in a heartbeat."

The door opened. Diamond tensed. Closed her eyes.

No Jackson.

They stepped into the darkened office area. Diamond drew short, erratic breaths. Her hands were clammy. Her heart beat a rhythm almost out of her chest. "Don't do this," she hissed.

"Shut up" was the whispered reply.

"Baby?" Jackson's footsteps sounded as he stepped off of a carpeted area onto the marbled hallways. "What are you—"

Jackson rounded the corner, took in the scene and found out that a man could still live when his heart stopped beating.

He stopped in his tracks, his face hard and unsmiling. Touching his woman alone was worth taking this fool's life. "Shay."

Diamond tried to move forward but Shay pulled her back. "Damn, dog. No smile, no hug? What kind of greeting is that for a brothah you haven't seen in a nickel and a dime?"

"Let her go, man. Whatever beef you have is with me, not her."

Shay tightened his grip, removed the gun from Diamond's

head and pointed it at Jackson. "You may think you're the boss, but I'm running this show. Now put your hands up and back into your office, nice and slow like."

"Shay…"

"Shut up and do what I tell you!"

Jackson looked at Diamond. Eyes filled with fear stared back at him and belied the calm demeanor she was trying so hard to convey. Shay placed the gun against Diamond's temple. "Back up!"

Jackson raised his hands and backed into his office. In his mind, his hands were around Shay's throat squeezing the life out of his former best friend's now worthless body. "Okay," he said, once they'd entered. "Now what?"

"At first, I was just going to kill you, but in the time it took me to get into this fortress you call an office, I've come up with another idea…call it a farewell gift from one friend to another. Here's how it's going to go down. You're going to sit down at that computer and conduct a little transfer. You're going to deposit a cool mil into this account." With the gun again in Diamond's back, and his eyes darting between her and Jackson, he reached into his pocket and pulled out a card. Jackson clenched his fists. "Don't move!" He prodded Diamond with the gun butt, over to Jackson's desk, where he laid down the card.

Then he jerked Diamond up against him, ran a hand over her body. Jackson clenched his jaw, took a step. Shay raised the gun to Diamond's head. Jackson froze. "And you, sexy, are going to do everything I tell you unless you want Boss to watch while I splatter your pretty brains all over the floor." The shiver was involuntary and Diamond cursed herself for her nervousness. Shay laughed, sinister and dark. "Damn, man. She's shaking and everything, like she loves you or something. What do you think, Boss," Shay taunted. "I'd say taking your woman and making her my sex slave, screwing her brains out and then passing her on to my friends just might make up for one or two of the almost twenty years you made me do."

Diamond struggled to break away. Shay laughed, rubbed the gun along her cheek.

He knew it was pointless to reason, but Jackson tried anyway. "Shay, we grew up together. You know me, man—"

"I thought I did."

"And you know I'd never rat you out. I've never been a snitch, man."

"Mighty funny then, that while me and Wesley both end up in prison, you don't even do a day in jail. If you didn't sing for the reward money or cooperate with the prosecutors, then how did that happen?"

"It happened because I didn't do anything, man. You know this!" Jackson took Shay's silence as a sign that he just might be listening. "Think about it, Shay. My uncle had hella paper. Why would I want ten lousy g's?"

"Oh, so you do remember that *lousy* amount offered as reward money." He took a quick look around. "Guess that's chump change to you now."

"Maybe Wesley tried to cut a deal, maybe that's how the prosecutor found the gun in the side panel."

"Well, now, wouldn't that be convenient considering the fact that he's dead!"

Donovan and Dexter pulled into the Boss Construction parking lot. One sentence was all Donovan needed to hear before they'd called the police and jumped into Dexter's Mercedes. Had there been any doubts that the car could indeed do 155 miles per hour, they'd definitely been put to rest on the drive over. Dexter killed the engine. As one, the brothers exited and walked across the lot, their steps steady and sure.

Donovan opened the door to the building. "The police said to wait for them."

Dexter shot his brother a look. "Yeah, right."

They stepped inside and rushed to the bank of elevators. Dexter pushed the button. The elevator dinged. Entering, he hurriedly pushed the button to the thirtieth floor. The light indicator blinked. "Damn!" He slammed his hand against the code panel, then looked at Donovan. "What are we going to do?"

Donovan was already heading out the elevator. "Stairs! Come on!"

Dexter was right behind him. "Won't the doors to the floors be locked?"

They reached the stairs and started to climb. "With our sister in danger on the other side of that door, it will take more than a lock to stop us."

"Man, I'm tired of talking. You've got five minutes to make the transfer."

"Shay, listen. I can't transfer this kind of money by computer. They have checks and balances on any transactions over ten thousand dollars. This transfer can only happen in person or over the phone."

Jackson watched Shay's finger slide to the trigger. He was surprised to find that the cool, calm, collected voice being heard in the room was his own. "Listen, Toe-2-Toe," Jackson continued, seeing a slight reaction at the use of his ex-friend's childhood name. "You don't want to do this, man. You just got out of prison. And you especially don't want to hurt somebody you've just met, who's never done anything to you. Let her go, man. Let this be between you and me."

Shay glanced at his watch. "Four minutes."

Jackson's mind spun with ways to thwart Shay's plan, for both him and Diamond to make it out of this mess alive.

"Look, I can transfer ten grand right now and set up the rest on Monday. It's the holidays, Shay, the banks are closed! Any more than ten thousand dollars won't go through! I can give you ten, you let her go, and then I'll lay low with you wherever you want until I can give you the rest." Belatedly, Jackson remembered the safe in his office. "Look, man. I've also got some cash here. In the safe behind that picture. Probably another ten g's or so. I'll give that to you, too."

Shay snorted. "Like you have a choice."

"This is your game, player." Jackson held up his hands in a sign of surrender.

"No! Get the cash out of the safe first."

Jackson watched Shay trail him over to where the safe was. "Just open it. Reach inside and your girl becomes a pleasant memory."

Jackson opened the safe and then stepped away, as Shay had commanded. "Get that money, sexy," Shay ordered Diamond, his voice becoming higher as his thrill increased. "Get me something to put this money in. No, Boss, you stay still. I'm talking to your bitch."

A curtain of fury came over Jackson. In spite of the gun, he began to walk toward Shay. "Disrespect my woman again," he said, his tone low and deadly, "and there won't be a gun big enough to keep me off your ass."

"We'll see about that," Shay responded, with a touch less bravado than before. He took the bag of money that Diamond handed him and then ordered Jackson over to the computer for the bank transaction.

Jackson sat down at the computer and picked up the card that Shay had laid on the desk. "This is too many numbers." He looked up. "This must not be a California account."

"Don't worry about where the money is going. Just know that I'll be meeting up with it soon and living the good life the way you've been doing for all these years."

Jackson began typing.

"Wait!" Shay moved himself and Diamond a bit closer to Jackson. "Turn that screen around so that I can see it. I need to make sure that you're depositing my money, not sending an email to the police." Shay laughed. It held no humor.

Jackson adjusted the computer and pulled up one of his smaller bank accounts. The balance showed just a little over one hundred thousand. He clicked a couple keys, put in the number Shay had given him, and within minutes, the screen showed that the transaction had been completed.

"There you go, man," Jackson said, leaning back as if re-laxing but actually gauging the distance between him and the gun. Could he make a lunge before Shay fired? "Ten thousand in your bank account with more where that came from on Monday. In fact, by doing the transfer in person I can get you two million. Because even though I had nothing to do with you going to prison, you're my friend from back in the—"

*Thud. Thud. Thud.*

Shay's head snapped around toward the sound.

Mere seconds of distraction. Just what the construction owner ordered. He pushed Diamond away from Shay while simultaneously reaching for the gun. His forward momentum caused the men to fall to the floor. Jackson tried to grab the weapon. Shay tried to fire it. They rolled and Jackson was on top. Diamond stood frozen, her eyes glued to Jackson's hand wrapped around Shay's hand, both gripping the gun. *Call the police!* But she couldn't move. Jackson almost had the gun away from Shay. *You've almost got it. Come on, baby!*

They rolled again. Now Shay was on top.

*Oh, no!*

The battle was for the aim of the gun—Shay pushing it down toward Jackson's head, Jackson forcing Shay's arm to the sky.

Finally, Diamond remembered how to move her legs. She

ran to the phone. But wait. *Is that a set of golf clubs over in the corner?* Acting on pure instinct, Diamond grabbed an iron and ran over to the fighting men. Jackson snatched the gun. A millisecond later Diamond channeled Tiger Woods and swung like she was trying to drop a hole in one from three hundred yards. Shay went down. Jackson jumped up and trained the gun on Shay. Even if his former homeboy had some fight left in him, he'd have to come to first.

Jackson rushed over to Diamond. "Baby." He hugged her tight against him even as he kept one eye trained on the non-moving hump lying on the floor. "I thought I was going to lose you."

Diamond couldn't talk past the lump in her throat. She buried her head into Jackson's chest, relishing the feel of him, the smell of him, the sound of his heartbeat.

Footsteps filled the silence. Dexter burst into the room. "Diamond!"

Donovan was right behind him. He took in the scene, most notably, Jackson and Diamond alive and well. The man on the floor, not so much. Shay moaned and Jackson immediately put Diamond behind him. He trained the gun on Shay's head. "Don't move."

More footsteps. The police. "Hands up! Get down on the ground. Down on the ground!"

A second officer spoke up. "That's Jackson Wright. He owns this place."

The other officers looked around, confused.

"Him." Jackson nodded toward Shay as he placed down the gun and leaned against his desk. The weight of what almost happened bore down on him, body and soul. "His name is Shay Thomas and he just tried to kill us. He's the one you want."

The police officers surrounded Shay and escorted him

out of the building to the tune of his Miranda rights. Neither Jackson nor Diamond saw him leave. They only had eyes for each other.

# Chapter 36

It was a little after midnight when the limousine carrying Jackson, Diamond, Dexter and Donovan turned into the grand entrance of the Drake Estate. In just twenty-four short hours the grounds had gone from a Thanksgiving haven to a winter wonderland. After four hours in a cramped police station, no one noticed. Rudolph with his red nose and his posse could have sideswiped them with Santa drinking Drake's finest, and they wouldn't have noticed. It had been one hell of a night.

"Baby," Diamond said, in yet another attempt to shift away from Jackson. "I'm getting a crick in my neck."

Jackson loosened his grip yet kept an arm around her shoulder. He'd barely been a hair's breadth away from her since Shay was taken away in cuffs. As if she were a mirage, a puff of smoke that would disappear if he let her go.

"Parents are here," Donovan said matter-of-factly when the front of their mansion came into view.

Dexter sighed. "Damn."

"I told them not to end their vacation!" Diamond said, pounding her fist on the car's soft leather.

"You know good and well Daddy wasn't going to hear what he heard, and see what he probably saw on TV, and keep chilling in Cabo."

They were bum-rushed as soon as they walked through the door.

"Diamond!" Genevieve rushed over to hug her daughter. Good luck while said jewel was glued to Jackson's side.

"Baby girl," Donald said, his voice gruff with emotion. He joined his wife and hugged his daughter, or tried to, anyway. But he actually hugged part of Diamond and all of Jackson's arm. "Do you mind?"

Jackson released her. Reluctantly. He stepped away a full six inches, saw an opening and placed a hand on top of Diamond's head. Yes, he did.

"Baby, we were so worried about you. The news said that the man was armed!" While Jackson's clout had managed to keep Diamond's name out of the story, all of the other details had somehow found their way onto "breaking news."

Donald gave a final squeeze and stepped back. "The only thing that matters is that you're okay."

"I'm fine, Daddy."

Warm and fuzzy left the room when Donald turned to Jackson. "You put my daughter in harm's way. She could have lost her life tonight because of whatever you're involved in."

"Dad, no—"

"Baby, it's all right," Jackson said, pulling up to his full six foot five while looking Donald dead in the eye. "I want to talk to your father."

"Good," Donald said. Clearly, this wasn't his first time at the rodeo. "We need to discuss this man-to-man."

"I agree." Jackson and Donald turned to leave the room.

Two strong men. Diamond envisioned another rumble. "Dad, wait."

"Let them go," Genevieve whispered. "They'll be all right."

Forty-five agonizing minutes later, Jackson rejoined Diamond, who was now alone in the great room. She rushed him as soon as he entered the room. "What happened? What did you say to my father?"

"I told him what happened." He reached for her hand.

Diamond held back. "Where are we going?"

Jackson sighed, the weight of what had almost happened, what he'd almost lost, still pressing him down. "I also told him that we'd see everyone in the morning. I'm tired, love. But I need you with me. Let's go home."

The average person wouldn't have noticed, but Jackson was still alert enough to discern the additions to security detail around his home: the camera attached to a phone pole a mile away and above his gate, a small red beam indicating a motion detector so sensitive that it would know when Molly Mosquito went to visit Nicholas Gnat. Once inside his estate, security was visible. Two guards were posted just inside the gate. Jackson knew that four more cased the perimeter of the ten-acre estate.

Diamond looked at the guards, and then at Jackson. "Is this necessary?"

Jackson shrugged. "Maybe, maybe not. But I'm not going to take a chance of you being endangered again. Got it?"

Diamond nodded.

They entered the sanctuary of Jackson's home and immediately felt more peaceful. As beautiful as the Drake Estate was, there was something about being near the water, hearing the waves crash against the shore, that soothed and comforted like no other sound. Diamond took off her shoes and stifled a yawn.

"Tired, baby?"

"After subduing a killer, being grilled by the police and then, even worse, Genevieve, and now seeing that it is 3:00 a.m.?" Diamond channeled the dry sarcasm her mother was known for to perfection. "Yeah, a little bit."

Jackson laughed, a sound that earlier in the evening he would have doubted he'd hear again. "I deserved that. I'm tired, too. But do you think you could take a shower with me?"

They entered the master suite, shed their clothes and were soon sitting on the marble bench in Jackson's massive shower. Water poured over them as they sat hugging each other, thankful to do so, thankful to be alive. As exhausted as she was, Diamond would have thought herself incapable of getting excited for physical pleasure, but Jackson's roaming hands were like a caffeine shot and within minutes he had her body humming like a bird.

He kissed her, softly, lovingly, on her temple—his favorite place besides his *other* favorite place—ear and cheek. One hand kneaded the back of her neck while the other sought and found an already taut nipple. He tweaked it, and at the same time he slanted his mouth over Diamond's and demanded entry with his tongue. Soon the twirling and sucking began—hot, wet—as if tasting each other for the first time. Strong arms enveloped Diamond as Jackson, spurred on by the knowledge that he'd almost lost this piece of paradise, deepened the kiss. His tongue plunged to the depths of her mouth, seemingly to the depths of her soul. He hardened immediately and completely, his engorged shaft now tickling Diamond's thighs.

She opened them, wanting him as much as he wanted her. Wanting to fill his width and length inside her, wanting him to stroke away the fear the day had brought and memories of what she'd almost lost. She wanted to be owned by him,

claimed by him, branded by him. She circled her hand around
his dick. "This," she whispered into his mouth. "I want this."

On the way over, Jackson had planned a tender scene of
seduction. Those plans flew out the window as his body, hot
and shaking with wanting, took over his mind. He needed
to be inside of this woman, now. Needed to be connected.
Needed to belong. Obviously Diamond was thinking the same
thing because she stood, positioned herself over his happy
stick and slowly, oh…so…slowly, sank down on his heat. She
groaned at how fully he filled her, even as her hips welcomed
this awesome intrusion by swirling around and around as she
rose up and down, over and again. She bent over, placed her
hands on the floor, giving Jackson a bird's-eye view of her
backside. The position heightened both of their pleasures, and
Jackson squeezed her sweet cheeks as he intensified the ride.
It was a beautiful symphony—the water, the rhythm, the delicious friction. It was too much, it wasn't enough. Jackson
wanted, no, *needed* to be closer, deeper. With one final swat
of her butt, he lifted her off him, stood and picked her up. Diamond's legs immediately went around his waist, giving him
unobstructed access to his destination. He placed her against
the wall and, looking deep into her eyes with more love than
Diamond thought possible from one being, sank into her yet
again. His hips and tongue were a concerto as they matched
rhythms: swirling, grinding, searching for the innermost of
places, that place untouched by anyone else. That place that
neither had ever felt before. He licked her neck, long, wet
strokes, and the combination of that and the relentless pounding happening below was a decadent combination that made
Diamond cry out with joy. Jackson moaned, burying himself
to the hilt and leaning them both against the wall to catch
their breaths.

But he wasn't finished. He was just getting started.

# Chapter 37

$S$till joined, he walked them over to one of the immense showerheads. "Hang on, baby," he said, when they stood directly beneath it. She grabbed ahold of the showerhead, he placed her legs over his shoulder, and there, totally exposed and at his mercy, Diamond began the ride of her life. Grabbing her hips, Jackson took over, became the maestro of their lovemaking as yet again he yielded thrust after powerful thrust, rotating her hips in time to his rhythm. Mewling sounds came to Diamond's ears. Belatedly, she realized it was she who was making them. She wrapped her arms around his broad shoulders and let Jackson own her, brand her, love her with an intensity she'd never thought possible. They climaxed together.

"Jackson!"

"Diamond!"

He eased her down, sat her on the bench. Washed her. Kissed her. Hugged her.

And still, he hadn't had enough of Diamond Drake.

After making quick work of his own shower, they walked into his suite. "Are you hungry?" he asked.

She realized she was starving.

"Come on. Let's see if Chef left anything tasty downstairs."

They raided the kitchen and soon returned to the master suite with Kobe roast beef sandwiches and a bottle of wine. When Diamond looked at the label she chided Jackson. "You'd better be glad you have mad lovemaking skills, otherwise you'd be in trouble for patronizing the competition!" Her words were only mildly serious; for the most part the neighboring vineyards were friendly and their wine up to snuff.

Jackson uncorked the bottle of 2010 Thornton Tempranillo and filled their glasses. They ate and recalled the evening.

"I don't think I've ever been as frightened as when I rounded the corner and saw that gun to your head."

"I don't think I've ever been as frightened as when I *felt* it at my head."

"I'm so sorry, baby."

"It wasn't your fault, Jackson. I think that Shay Thomas has had it out for you a long time, maybe even when you thought he was your friend. The look of hate that I saw in his eyes…" Diamond shuddered. "I've never been that close to pure evil."

Jackson smiled. "You held your own, though. I've been calling you a BAP but I had that shit twisted. Underneath those designer duds and painted nails was a ride-or-die chick." Diamond swatted him playfully. Jackson laughed and took her in his arms. "My ride-or-die chick," he whispered, as he placed kisses all over her face. "I love you, girl."

Soon their hunger for each other replaced their need of food. They finished their glasses of wine. Jackson lit a fire in the marble fireplace that anchored the suite. Diamond lay down on the faux fur in front of it. She sighed in contentment as she watched Jackson walk around the room in all his naked glory. Michelangelo could not have sculpted a finer work of art. He lit candles, set his iPod to a selection of love songs and, once he felt he'd set a proper mood, joined Diamond in front of the roaring fire.

This time, their lovemaking was slow, deliberate, the way Jackson had originally intended. He turned his body so that his head was at her toes and then he lovingly sucked one into his mouth. Who knew that making love to one's feet could be so stimulating? Diamond found out, and soon she'd scooted her body down to where her mouth was in line with one of her favorite parts of Jackson's body. She wet her lips and took in as much of his burgeoning erection as possible. Jackson's groan was low and deep as she licked and sucked, nibbled and tasted. Not one to be outdone, Jackson spread her legs and dove headfirst into her wetness. He tickled her nub with his tongue, flicked it into life until it was a pebbled hardness between her legs. He licked her thoroughly, everywhere, in every way. They used their bodies to communicate the love that words alone could not convey. As the vestiges of dawn streaked across the sky in orange, pink and purple hues, Jackson once again plunged deep inside her, stroking her into yet another frenzy. He was insatiable. He was a beast! Diamond matched him stroke for stroke, loving every minute. She felt him wholly inside her, as if touching her very soul. She felt his love not only in body, but in spirit. This time, as she cried out, tears of happiness rolled down her face.

"You all right, baby?" He reached for a couple nearby pillows and, still lying on the fur, cuddled Diamond spoon-style in his arms.

"I'm perfect," Diamond answered. "I never thought I could

feel this way." She turned to look at him, her eyes wide and searching. "Is this real, baby? Or is this a dream?"

"I don't know," he replied, playfully flicking her nose with his finger. "But if it is, then please don't wake me up."

And that's how Diamond went to sleep: sated, naked, and in Jackson's arms. As soon as he was sure she slept soundly, Jackson got up and went online, searching for the perfect thank-you gift for Diamond saving his life. An hour later he'd found what he was looking for and, after a series of phone calls, was ensured that a delivery would be made the following morning at the place of his instruction.

The next day, Jackson and Diamond arrived at the Drake Estate in time for Saturday brunch. On a self-prescribed vacation from cooking for the holidays, Genevieve had called upon David and Mary's chef to prepare for the festivities. The table was laden with brunch favorites: pecan waffles, eggs Benedict, home-style potatoes and breakfast meats. Pitchers of mimosas completed the menu, made with fresh-squeezed orange juice and a Drake sparkling chardonnay. The only thing more plentiful than the food was the laughter. At their bequest, Jackson and Diamond had shared the details of their hazardous adventure as Papa Dee, David Jr., Mary, Donald, Genevieve, Donovan and Dexter looked on.

"Your daughter is gangster," Jackson said to Donald, as he reached for another strip of crispy bacon. "She handled that nine-iron like a pro!"

"Glad to see those golf lessons counted for something," Donald grumbled.

"Y'all don't know nothing 'bout gangster," Papa Dee said, his ninety-eight-year-old eyes twinkling with laughter and life. "Did I tell you about the time when I was twenty and I outran Al Capone and his gang?"

"No, Dad," David Jr. said, "but I think we're getting ready to hear the tale."

Just then, Jackson received a phone call. "I'm sorry, but this is business," he said upon rising. "I'll make it as brief as possible."

It was almost fifteen minutes before Jackson returned. Diamond's eyes asked the obvious—*where have you been?*

"Later" was the one-word response Jackson whispered in her ear.

As brunch neared its end, Donald stood. "I'd like to propose a toast. I'd like to once again thank God that Jackson and Diamond are safe. And I'd like to say cheers to the new Drake posse!"

Laughter abounded amid the cheers.

Jackson stood. "I'd like to propose a toast, also, if I may." The room quieted. "Yesterday when I saw the gun against Diamond's head, *my* life flashed before my eyes. Because in that moment I realized just how much she meant to me and how much I didn't want to lose her. In the short time I've known all of you, and for the first time since my adoptive parents died, I've felt the bond of family. I want to thank you for welcoming me into your home and your lives, and if Diamond will have me, I'd like to become a part of this family forever." Jackson got down on one knee. "This is the business I was handling just now, baby. Dealing with the contact who dropped off this package."

Diamond's eyes widened in disbelief as her hand slowly lifted to cover her open mouth. *No, this isn't happening. This man is not proposing to me!*

But he was.

"Diamond, I love you. You are more precious than your namesake, more valuable than any jewel. I didn't know true love until you walked into my life and I'll never know true love again without you. You saved my life, baby, in more ways than one. Will you do me the immense honor of becoming my wife? Will you marry me?"

He reached into his pocket, pulled out a blue box, opened it and, amid gasps and sounds of impressed approval, placed a perfectly designed five-carat, princess-cut Tiffany diamond on her finger.

The room held its breath.

Diamond smirked. "What? No rooster?"

"Rooster?" Papa Dee exclaimed. "What is that child talking about?"

"It's a private joke," Jackson replied, his smile slight as he continued to gaze intently at Diamond, waiting for her answer.

"Well, go on, girl," Dexter prodded. "Don't keep the man hanging all day!"

Diamond could barely speak for the tears. "Yes!" she finally whispered. "A thousand times, yes!" she continued with increased volume. She leaned over and hugged the love of her life.

He stood, picked her up and twirled them around. "I love you, Diamond Drake."

Diamond placed a soft kiss on his mouth. "I love you, Boss."

And as her family applauded, Diamond recognized two things—with big risks came big rewards, and dreams? They really could come true.

* * * * *

NATIONAL BESTSELLING AUTHOR

# ROCHELLE ALERS

*Private* **PASSIONS**

Successful journalist Emily Kirkland never expected that
her longtime friendship with gubernatorial candidate
Christopher Delgado would result in their secret
marriage. Now, with scandal and a formidable enemy
threatening their most cherished dreams, Emily must
uncover the truth, risking all for a passion
that could promise forever....

"The characters have depth, a strong sense of compassion
and loyalty... A fine book!"

—*RT Book Reviews* on *Private Passions*

*Available the first week of April 2012 wherever books are sold.*

KIMANI PRESS™

**www.kimanipress.com**

KPRA4740412

*Love can be
a risky business…*

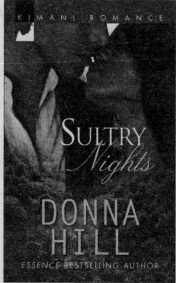

*Essence*
**bestselling author**
# DONNA HILL

## Sultry *Nights*

Dominique Lawson lives life on her own terms. But Trevor Jackson seems immune to her charms. That's until Dominique plots her all-out sensual assault on him. Dominique may be his boss, but Trevor plans to show the pampered princess what desire is really about. It's only a matter of time before the blue-blooded beauty is his—for all the sensual nights to come.

# LAWSONS *of* LOUISIANA

*Coming the first week of April 2012
wherever books are sold.*

www.kimanipress.com

KPDH2520412

*Score one for passion!*

*Pleasure*
**RUSH**

*Favorite author*
**FARRAH ROCHON**

In Hawaii, Deirdre Smallwood vows to shed her humdrum image and do something totally out of character: seduce former flame Thelonius Stokes. Theo is shocked by the uninhibited lover warming his bed. Deirdre is giving him a rush of pleasure he's never felt before. This time around, Theo vows to score on the only playing field that counts: the arena of love.

**KIMANI HOTTIES**
*It's All About Our Men*

*Available the first week of April 2012
wherever books are sold.*

**www.kimanipress.com**

KPFR2540412

*Kissing in the courtroom...*

To *Love* You *More*

## WAYNE JORDAN

Sexy-as-sin attorney George Simpson is as commanding in the courtroom as he is in his candlelit bedroom. But Rachel Davis can't believe what a playboy her first love has become. Seeing George again sends her heart into overdrive. Will her confessions of the past lead to a trial by fire...or a verdict of intimate seduction?

**"The hero and heroine heal in ways that anyone can relate to, making readers want to root for them."**

**—RT Book Reviews on MIDNIGHT KISSES**

*Available the first week of April 2012 wherever books are sold.*

www.kimanipress.com

KPWJ2550412

# REQUEST YOUR FREE BOOKS!

## 2 FREE NOVELS
## PLUS 2 FREE GIFTS!

KIMANI™ ROMANCE

### Love's ultimate destination!

**YES!** Please send me 2 FREE Kimani™ Romance novels and my 2 FREE gifts (gifts are worth about $10). After receiving them, if I don't wish to receive any more books, I can return the shipping statement marked "cancel." If I don't cancel, I will receive 4 brand-new novels every month and be billed just $4.94 per book in the U.S. or $5.49 per book in Canada. That's a saving of at least 21% off the cover price. It's quite a bargain! Shipping and handling is just 50¢ per book in the U.S. and 75¢ per book in Canada.* I understand that accepting the 2 free books and gifts places me under no obligation to buy anything. I can always return a shipment and cancel at any time. Even if I never buy another book, the two free books and gifts are mine to keep forever.

168/368 XDN FEJR

| | |
|---|---|
| Name | (PLEASE PRINT) |

| | |
|---|---|
| Address | Apt. # |

| | | |
|---|---|---|
| City | State/Prov. | Zip/Postal Code |

Signature (if under 18, a parent or guardian must sign)

### Mail to the **Reader Service:**

**IN U.S.A.:** P.O. Box 1867, Buffalo, NY 14240-1867
**IN CANADA:** P.O. Box 609, Fort Erie, Ontario L2A 5X3

Not valid for current subscribers to Kimani Romance books.

**Want to try two free books from another line?**
**Call 1-800-873-8635 or visit www.ReaderService.com.**

* Terms and prices subject to change without notice. Prices do not include applicable taxes. Sales tax applicable in N.Y. Canadian residents will be charged applicable taxes. Offer not valid in Quebec. This offer is limited to one order per household. All orders subject to credit approval. Credit or debit balances in a customer's account(s) may be offset by any other outstanding balance owed by or to the customer. Please allow 4 to 6 weeks for delivery. Offer available while quantities last.

**Your Privacy**—The Reader Service is committed to protecting your privacy. Our Privacy Policy is available online at www.ReaderService.com or upon request from the Reader Service.

We make a portion of our mailing list available to reputable third parties that offer products we believe may interest you. If you prefer that we not exchange your name with third parties, or if you wish to clarify or modify your communication preferences, please visit us at www.ReaderService.com/consumerschoice or write to us at Reader Service Preference Service, P.O. Box 9062, Buffalo, NY 14269. Include your complete name and address.

KROM11B

## Harlequin Desire

ALWAYS POWERFUL, PASSIONATE AND PROVOCATIVE.

**NEW YORK TIMES AND USA TODAY
BESTSELLING AUTHOR**

# BRENDA JACKSON

**PRESENTS A BRAND-NEW
WESTMORELAND FAMILY NOVEL!**

# FEELING THE HEAT

Their long-ago affair ended abruptly and
Dr. Micah Westmoreland knows Kalena Daniels
hasn't forgiven him. But now that they're working
side by side, he can't ignore the heat between them…
and this time he plans to make her his.

**Also available as a 2-in-1 that includes
*Night Heat*.**

*Available in April wherever books are sold.*